author

Connie's Silver Shoes

The Candy Cane Girls, book 4

By Bonnie Engstrom

Published by Forget Me Not Romances, a division of Winged Publications

ISBN-10:1-944203-51-6

ISBN-13:978-1-944203-51-1

Dedication

This book is dedicated to my six beautiful grandchildren, Taylor, Teagan, Fletcher, Shayden, Shyla and Huxley. Although they are not mentioned in this story, they had shining parts in others. I prayed for many years to be a grandmother, and I was blessed with what our family jokingly calls the explosion.

I also want to dedicate this book to Jill Stroope who was an exceptional wedding coordinator and who became an exceptional friend. Without her none of the weddings in the Candy Cane Series would have come to beautiful fruition, nor the ones of my own children. I am so sorry she retired, but I hope she will write her fascinating memoirs.

Bonnie Engstrom

ABOUT THE CANDY CANES

Special thanks to

* Jaeda Wayman for allowing me to feature him as the hero in this story. Yes, he does sometimes wear a dark red shirt, he is from New York (the city, not the country – hey, it's fiction), he does work for a large banking corporation, and he is a wonderful man. As of this writing, he has not yet read his own fictional story, but he will get a signed copy soon.

* Samantha at North Scottsdale Floral and Corinne Lewis at Elegance At Its Finest Floral Designs and her colleague Steve. I hope I described the wedding flowers the way they suggested and guided me. If you want to see Connie's bouquet, go to https://www.thebridalflower.com/product/gray-and-ivory-lovelie-gray-wedding-bouquet/.

* My daughter, Dana, who does all my social media posting, including my newsletter, *Life on the Lake*. (You can sign up for it at my website.) A busy mom of four children she somehow makes time for me. She is a true blessing.

* My wonderful and patient publisher Cynthia Hickey, owner of Forget Me Not Romances, a division of Winged Publications. She designs all my book covers, and I love the cover for Connie's Silver Shoes featuring my real, sadly deceased, Miniature Pincher, Jake.

* It goes without saying my husband Dave who prepares yummy meals while I write makes it possible for all my books to come to fruition.

* I don't know why I always wait until last to honor

Him, but Jesus my savior is really the one I write for, the one who inspired me to write and gave me the courage to do it. Without my faith in Him and my love for Him, there would be no books. I pray because of Him my books will touch hearts and draw readers to Him.

.

About Newport Beach

My family and I lived there for over thirty years, so it is close to my heart. We visited Balboa and The Pavilion many times. I remember at one time it did have Friday and Saturday night dancing. It has a long and checkered fascinating history and is now a designated California State Historic Landmark. Check out the website below to see fun photos of then and now, as well as two people I had the privilege to meet personally; Evelyn Hart, a former mayor, and Marion Bergeson, a former California state senator.

http://www.balboapavilion.com/

Bonnie Engstrom

CONNIE'S SILVER SHOES

CANES ABOUT THE CANDY CANES

This is book number four in the Candy Cane girls' series, but it, as all the others before and in future (yes, there will be more) can be read as a standalone. It might be more fun to start with Noelle's story in *Noelle's Christmas Wedding* and progress to Cindy's story in *Cindy's Perfect Dance*, but Natalie and Candy will explain everything about the Candy Canes to you in *Candy's Wild Ride*.

Over ten years ago six high school freshmen formed a swim team that became legendary. They won the state relay swim championship four years in a row. In addition to their skill and devotion to daily practicing, they prayed together and vowed to be sisters forever. Another thing that set them apart was they chose their own swimsuits making them a team within a larger team. They chose red and white diagonally striped swim suits. Thus, became known as the Candy Canes. They always will be.

I hope you enjoy their stories.

PROLOGUE

Connie gazed up at the sign above the glass window. *Winning Designs ~ Unique Custom Fashion Attire.*

She and Jaeda had prayed about which scripture to put underneath it. Finally, they compromised putting one below the name and one on the plate glass door next to the picture window displaying the headless mannequins and the little stuffed toy dog draped in plaid fabrics.

Philippians 4:13 was inscribed below the Winning Designs sign. It was her favorite verse, one she had always clung to when she swam on the high school swim team and when she started her business life. Yes, she *could* do all things through Christ. She could.

Jaeda's favorite was also one many people

would recognize. *"For everyone who asks receives; the one who seeks finds; and to the one who knocks, the door will be opened." Luke 11:10* It was followed underneath by the invitation *Knock and it will be opened.* There was no bell to ring.

They hugged each other, kissed, and opened the heavy glass door.

Soon, Doreen would become manager when they moved to their other home in Scottsdale.

CHAPTER ONE

*C*onnie hated male models. Always so full of themselves. The new one Doug introduced her to at the event tonight would definitely be trouble. He was Mr. Ego personified, always smoothing his wavy hair and glancing in everything glass he passed – not just mirrors, but glass front cabinets, even the glass top on the serving buffet.

She kicked her uncomfortable shoes off and threw them against her bedroom wall – hard. She laughed when one shoe made a thump and the other landed upside down on her carpet. Such extravagance – Michael Kors. She should have invested in the silver Italian ones for about the same money. But, Doug her boss, the founder of Nature's Designs, insisted on the ones with the gold heels and buckle. She had her own designer line now; yet Doug still called the shots when she had to make an appearance at a function.

As well as the ads with the models.

Poor Doreen – being subjected to a You Tube add about Connie's designs for the physically challenged in a demeaning way. Connie had wanted all adds – print, You Tube and social media, to be enlightening and positive.

She picked up her cell she had flung in anger on the bed. Doreen answered sobbing.

CHAPTER TWO

$\mathcal{T}$he Candy Cane sisters gathered at the Cannery

Restaurant for their annual pre-Christmas luncheon. All except Cindy now living in Costa Rica, and Candy who was on her honeymoon in Catalina Island. Connie looked around at four faces, Doreen, Natalie, Melanie and Noelle. Why did they look worried? Was her makeup smeared?

Noelle rose first from across the table to hug her. The others followed. She knew she hadn't exactly honored their special friendship pact when she dated Bill Lord Junior the Harley model. Still, she felt loved and wanted. That's what being a Candy Cane did. How blessed they all were to have been on the special swim team almost eleven years ago at Vista del Mar High School. Sometimes she'd heard comments like "Only in Newport Beach – so privileged." But, she knew better; she knew how hard they had worked and the bond they had formed in high school as freshmen, and the winning state swim team championship four years in a row. It would have been the same in Timbuctoo, special friends who loved and depended on each other, and prayed.

"Oysters!" Natalie exclaimed as the waiter approached. She was notorious for excessively imbibing in them. They all laughed.

"I," Doreen announced, "will have the chopped salad." All heads turned. "Yep, gotta watch my model's figure."

Connie felt guilty. She had gotten Doreen the modeling assignment because of her shorter leg after Melanie had caused the accident. She knew Melanie was forgiven both by God and Doreen, but was Doreen really happy being a gimp model? She asked.

"How do you feel about the ads Doug the Dog is producing?" She loved to call him that when not in his presence. A secretive way she could put her boss in his place.

"I'm okay with them. Not thrilled, but if it helps others with compromised or missing limbs and promotes your line, I am … okay." She winked at Connie, although her eyes were blurry.

"Okay is not good enough, Doreen." Connie said. "We need to talk later."

~

Doreen led the way almost tripping down the ramp from the restaurant in her special shoe. She seemed anxious to get out of there. The other girls followed.

Noelle spoke first. "Connie, Doreen, can you please send those You Tube ads to me? I want to see them."

Doreen shook her head, but Connie nodded. Noelle being a teacher, especially an English one, had good insight about language and content. She had written a local education column while still in college. Connie would value her advice. She would forward the You Tubes to her tomorrow.

~

Connie fretted. Fretting was not her style. Although not very astute at remembering Bible verses, somehow Psalm 37 came to mind. That, and Joyce Meyer's devotion she'd read this morning. She looked up the chapter on her cell's Bible ap. Several verses advised against fretting. They would help her get through the day with courage and present her case to Doug.

She was grateful for her association with him and Nature's Designs. She believed God had led her there. But, during the past few years, Doug had changed perspective. When he first started the company he seemed to be all about supporting designs made only with natural products, no synthetics. Now, he was more about money.

Connie understood that it was business, and she was a part of it. But, couldn't the two be combined? Doug had managed to insert himself and the company into a big conglomerate. Now, it was the defining factor. Connie hated it. She wanted her own design business, based on her beliefs of Christian ethics. But, how? She was a small guppy in a big tank. Frustrated, she called Natalie who was known as the organized and sensible one of the group.

"Maybe, Nat, you will have some ideas for me. If not, at least let me vent."

Natalie prayed with Connie as all Candy Canes did with each other. When she said "Amen," she shared an idea.

"I think you need to talk with Bill Lord, Vivian's husband, Candy's new step-father. He is a super business person and always has ideas."

~

Bill was excited. He loved new ideas, especially from young entrepreneurs. This is what he believed in, what he wanted to encourage. Few people knew he was part of The Memory Men group that financed businesses anonymously. It was top secret. All transactions were moved through a local bank. Only one bank officer was privy to the names in the group. He was sure he could trust Jaeda.

~

Bill Lord and she had met at Starbucks, and she shared. Now, she was looking in the mirror above her dresser.

Connie mopped her eyes with the backs of her fists. So embarrassing to share with Bill Lord. But, she did it. She hadn't known she could have so much courage to bare her heart and dump all her insecurities at his feet. She looked in the mirror and swiped concealer around her puffy eyes, then blinked rapidly. Isn't that what models were told to do to make their eyes glisten? She picked up the business card Bill had given her to slip into her bag. Jaeda. What an interesting name. Hopefully he would be a person who could help her.

~

Jaeda put the phone down slowly. Such an unusual call from Bill Lord who was adamant about secrecy. He knew Bill was the founder and head of the Memory Men group. They had met initially when Lord was forming the group and explained their mission. That was almost five years ago. They had never had any individual contact since. Not in person, not in writing, nor on the phone. So, why now?

Bill asked him to meet with a talented young

woman, a clothing designer – or was it called couture? Maybe fashion was a better word. He often groped with proper adjectives. Math and money were his strengths. Jaeda tapped his pen on the glass top of his desk. Sometimes that helped him think, just as drumming on his African djembe drum did. It and the bi-monthly drum circles he'd attended had been a big bone of contention with Keona. Drumming hadn't really caused their breakup, but it helped. Fortunately, his little Min Pin accepted it. Jake's ears would stand up in peaks, and once he actually started to dance on his hind legs, ballerina style. Now, he really was Jaeda's best friend. Even slept with him which Keona never allowed. Fortunately, the dog's twelve pounds didn't take up too much room in the king bed.

The Connie woman called for an appointment. Today at three in the afternoon. Jaeda had no idea what she looked like, but Bill Lord had explained the Candy Cane group enough that he figured she was at least pretty. He straightened his mini-print tie, checked the cuff links in his dark red starched shirt and ran a hand over his shaved head. Maybe he would think about a moustache. Maybe next week.

He was unprepared for Connie when she walked in. Talk about beautiful. Her chestnut hair streaked with natural blonde highlights was cut in a flippant style, just grazing her jawbones. Her smile was shaky. Did she have any actual idea why she was here?

Jaeda extended his hand and hoped his smile was warm. He liked her immediately when he felt her firm handshake. Connie smiled, and her face lit up showing sparkling azure eyes that reminded him of the ocean at morning break. The color of her dark red lips matched his shirt. Silly comparison. But, they did.

He indicated the chair across from him and settled in the chair behind his desk. She spoke first. "I – I'm not sure why I am here. Are you?"

Jaeda nodded, but asked a silent prayer for the right words. He mustn't give away the secret, so he had to be discreet. Normally, he didn't clear his throat before speaking with a client, but, this was a unique situation. Was she a client? Or, was Bill Lord the actual client. *Please, God, guide me.*

"I am a bit mystified, too. But, I will share what I do know," he said. "There is a group of investors in Newport Beach who give start-up funds to young entrepreneurs." He looked to her for confirmation.

"I've heard of that, but I don't know anyone in the group. Do you?"

He avoided the question. "It's secretive. Their names are very private. Protects them, I guess, from people tapping them for support." She looked at him quizzically, beautiful eyebrows raised.

"But, why would Mr. Lord suggest I have a meeting with you? Doesn't make sense," she said.

"He must know."

"I'm guessing he has some connection," he said trying to avoid lying. How could he get around this without jeopardizing Lord, or himself? "He probably knows someone in the group, but has been sworn to secrecy." Well, he does 'know' himself. Guess that explanation will have to do. He folded his hands together and brought them to his chin. Maybe that attentive gesture would put her at ease.

~

Connie shook Jaeda's hand and blew out about ten breaths on the way to her car. This group of investors wanted to help her. Unbelievable. She wiped the sweat off her palms and slid into the seat of her little car. Bill Lord must have some fancy connections. Should she call him and thank him, or was his involvement part of the secret? Right now she couldn't get Jaeda's handsome face out of her brain. She noticed his attire – spiffy and modern, not too over stated. She had looked casually at the other bank manager types, but their clothes were boring, too conservative. Jaeda's was conservative, but with personal touches like the dark red shirt and cuff links. Who wore cuff links anymore? Not since the sixties.

~

Bill was helping Vivian with the salad when his business cell buzzed. She was on a salad kick diet, and he was fine with it. At their ages they needed to watch their weight. But, he did crave bread. He was rewarded when she topped the chopped salad with slices of chicken breast and set a plate of warm olive bread on the table. Still, he was looking forward to the wedge of dark chocolate he would slip into his mouth after dinner.

He let the phone go to voicemail. He would check it later.

CHAPTER THREE

*C*onnie drove past the Nature's Designs warehouse office and around the block three times. She slapped her cheek, shook her head and, finally, clapped her hands laughing. She giggled so hard she almost ran up on the curb. *Oops! Better pay attention to driving. But, I can't believe it, just can't. Is it true, Lord? Will I really have my own design studio? Control over my own ads? My own business? How will I tell Doug? Who is my benefactor? So many questions.*

Doreen was on a pedestal getting a fitting. She was facing a grimy window when she saw Connie's car. Again, and again. Was something wrong? Why did she keep passing the office?

"Excuse me," she said to Alice the seamstress pining the hem of her skirt. "I need to make an important call." She stepped off the pedestal, grabbed her purse from a nearby chair and reached for her phone. Punching in Connie's number, she waited. Why wasn't she answering?

Connie heard her phone buzz. She had put it on silent for when she had the meeting with the banker, the Jaeda guy. She would check her messages later when she calmed down. She was such a wreck. Who were these people offering to provide her with her own design studio, and pay for all the advertising? How did they know her? How did they even know her gifts and abilities? So mysterious. She thought back to what Jaeda had suggested. "Find a place for your studio," he'd said. "First things first."

She was at a total loss. Then she remembered Rob and Braydon Lovejoy's father was a mega real estate agent. Maybe he could help. She didn't know where else to turn, so she called Logan Lovejoy.

~

Mr. Lovejoy was very kind and suggested they meet for coffee. Tomorrow would be fine. They met at the Starbucks in Corona del Mar. He asked a lot of questions, some of which she had a feeling he knew the answers to. But, how would he?

He poured his double Americano into a mug he

bought. "I hate to drink out of paper, and besides Lydia collects these. Silly, huh?" He slid his chair back and grabbed a pretty green mug handing it to Connie. "One for you, too." His grin put Connie at ease.

"Oh, no, I couldn't. I should be buying you coffee and mugs." Logan shook his head, removed the plastic dome from Connie's Frappuccino and poured her drink into the ceramic cup.

"Lydia will be thrilled – two more to add to her frivolous collection. Now, tell me all. How did all this transpire? Start at the beginning."

Connie swallowed her embarrassment with her next sip of coffee. "It was sort of out of the blue. I've been frustrated with being one of many designers for Doug's company. I was belly aching to Natalie when she convinced me to call Mr. Lord Senior. I guess he put some wheels in motion for me to meet with a handsome bank employee, Jaeda." She paused to make sure he was paying attention. He seemed to be gazing beyond her, above her head. Was she talking too much, too fast?

"Go on. What did this Jaeda say?"

"I was as nervous as a fish out of its tank. I'm not sure I remember every word, or every detail. But, I'm pretty sure he said a group of investors who support young entrepreneurs wanted to back me with …." She named what to her was an astronomical sum and felt her eyes glisten. Logan

Lovejoy nodded. "Then he told me 'first things first. Find a place for your studio.'"

Logan tapped the side of his mug. "Have you thought about location? Location is all, especially for a business."

Connie shook her head. She felt so dumb struck, so dumb, actually.

"Where, if you could chose anywhere in Newport, would you want to be?"

"I'm so used to the Peninsula and the Balboa area. But, there isn't much exposure there. What would you suggest?"

"Do you like Corona del Mar?"

"Oh, love it! Could never afford it. Why?"

"I don't do many rentals, but an interesting one just came on the market near Love In Bloom, Lydia's floral shop." He looked at her face for a reaction. Her smile quivered. "Not totally out of your league, your new league, Connie. It's a unique situation, and if you want we can scoot by there and check it out."

Did she ever! She slid into the passenger seat of Logan's SUV, somewhat surprised it wasn't a Mercedes. Why had she even thought that?

He parked behind Love In Bloom in a free space in the alley and led her through the back door of the shop. She stopped to hug Braydon who gave her a pink rose bloom. So far, even if this place didn't pan out, it was a fun mini journey. These folks were like family to her and all the Candy Canes. They chatted for a few minutes, Braydon catching her up on Rob and Cindy in Costa Rica, and she told him the little she knew about Candy and Devin's honeymoon in Catalina. She held the pink rose up to her nose and followed Logan out the door.

~

Connie sat on her bed shivering. Not from cold, but from excitement. Her whole life, her whole world seemed to be changing almost overnight. She had signed a lease contract for the studio with Logan negotiating. He was so well respected the other realtor never batted an eye, just nodded. She could hardly believe she would not only have her own studio in Corona del Mar, but she would be living above it in a darling apartment. Logan would put her little house in Costa Mesa on the market as a rental which would give her more monthly income.

He told her to make a list. She grabbed a handy piece of paper, then decided to boot up Word on her laptop. That way she could switch items around or delete them.

* Models (need Doreen if she doesn't have a binding contract with Doug. Need male models. Ugh.)
* Furniture (for apartment and studio)
* Seamstress (es) for measuring models and

cutting/sewing the designs and altering – Alice?

* Advertising. That was a tough one. She needed someone with expertise to design print and media ads, as well as someone to do front signage, maybe press releases, too.

So overwhelming! How could she do all this? She needed the advice of the Candy Canes.

~

"How did it go with Connie?" Lydia smiled at the two mugs and put them in the dishwasher. She was thrilled for Connie when Logan explained it all, but a bit worried, too. "She's pretty green at this, isn't she?"

"I agree. But, I think if the bank guy, Jaeda, guides her, she will be fine." He scratched his head. "Do we know him? I don't remember Bill Lord mentioning his name before. Or, I may have met him briefly once long ago."

"I don't think so, but Bill must trust him or he wouldn't have sent Connie to him."

~

Jaeda settled himself behind his glass-topped desk and felt his face light up. That beautiful designer girl, Connie, sat in the chair opposite. He loved the creative types, especially the ones with flawless skin and sparkling ocean blue eyes. His mother would have a fit if she knew he was attracted to a fair skinned girl, and a designer, yet!

Keona was another matter, not that it was any of her business anymore. Their divorce was finalized last month. He had boarded Jake at the vet's and celebrated with a long ride to Arizona on his Yamaha R1. He fell in love with Scottsdale, so much like Newport. Fancy cars, great restaurants, fun sports and entertainment venues, and that Go AZ motorcycle place. Unbelievable with a huge underground area filled with nearly a thousand cycles.

He had splurged on one of the best hotels, The Westin Kierland, just a mile from the Kierland shopping center. More great restaurants and upscale shops. Maybe he should ask for a transfer.

Connie tilted her head. Was Jaeda in this galaxy? He seemed so far away. Finally, he rubbed a palm across his forehead and smiled. "Sorry. Got distracted. Not professional. Now, how can I help you?"

"Not sure. One of my mentors suggested I speak with you for advice. Like maybe how to divvy up this wonderful windfall I came into. How to budget it. Think you can help?"

He looked her account up on his computer and pulled out a calculator. Why was he so distracted? She was just another bank client. Then she smiled, and she was more than that.

CHAPTER FOUR

She hadn't called Doreen back. Guilt and confusion clogged her mind. What kind of friend was she? She dialed.

"Oh, Con, I was so worried about you." Doreen sounded like she was about to burst into tears. "Why did you keep driving back and forth in front of the warehouse?"

"I was trying to process something unbelievable and wonderful." She finally had the gumption to share. Doreen hooted.

"I am doing a Snoopy dance for you. Can you hear me?"

Connie laughed with joy. So special to have

23

another Candy Cane share it. She knew she was getting a bit ahead of herself, and of the financial calendar she and Jaeda had planned, but she couldn't resist. After all, she had gotten Doreen into this crazy design business, and she was the primary model for the disability line. Without Doreen, that line wouldn't have existed in Connie's design collection. Now, it was getting bigger.

~

She needed to call her mom.

Connie envied Candy's and Noelle's relationships with their moms. She loved her mom, but she had never felt close enough to share deep secrets with her. Not even joys. Mabel Winfield always reacted the same to sad and joyful news. Eyebrows arched, she would pull her glasses down low on her nose and quote a Bible verse. Usually one about sin. She seldom got excited, and more often seemed to display disapproval. Like when Connie told her after the graduation ceremony from college in design with a 3.8 that she planned to pursue her dream.

It hadn't done any good to explain the less than 4.0 was because of the dreaded science classes she was forced to take. Biology and botany lent little to creativity. She had loved the History of Design, and embraced all the art classes. The information in those easily conveyed to fashion design.

Mom had just shaken her head, patted her on

the shoulder and said a simple "Congrats." No "I'm proud of you," not "You worked so hard." She hadn't even given Connie flowers or a gift, just a card with a simple pre-printed message signed Mom and Dad. It could have been a card for anyone.

Dad had been great, though, hugging her close, whispering how proud he was of her in her ear, maybe so Mom wouldn't hear his sentiments. Then right in front of all the robed graduates and their guests he swung her in a dance routine. Onlookers clapped, smiled and cheered. Mom turned and walked away. "Come on, George. Stop being ridiculous."

She knew her sister Sandra (always pronounced Sawn-dra, Mom insisted) felt bad for her. She had frowned at Mom's retreating back, touched their dad on the shoulder and said, "Daddy, we had better go." But, the words were soft and said in kindness. Then she smiled and winked at Connie after she touched her arm lightly.

Connie still felt Sandra's feathery touch of pride on her arm almost five years later. She touched the place now, and her eyes filled with unshed tears. Blinking hard, she pulled her phone out of her giant purse and pressed the number for Denver. Maybe, if she was lucky, Dad would answer so she could tell him her good news first.

~

Jaeda squeezed the bridge of his nose. He was

worried about the budget he and Connie had done. Land O' Goshen, he hoped he was wrong. The ancient phrase his grandmother used to use popped into his head unbidden and made him chuckle. Hopefully, there was some humor in his concern. He gestured to Rita the manager in the glassed cubicle across from him. He'd always thought he was more than decent in math, but Rita had the reputation among the other bank managers as "The Whiz." She pulled a chair up next to him while he explained.

"Right here," she said pointing a blue-tipped finger at the entry line about housing. He hoped she couldn't see the blush on his dark skin, but she must have. "Don't be embarrassed, Jae. It's a common mistake. But, I do think you should get in touch with her before she overextends herself in that area. Unless she already has."

He hoped not. He dialed Connie's number right away. Busy. He guessed she probably saw she was getting another call, but couldn't interrupt the one she was on. Text.

Need to talk. Important. Call me, please. ASAP

It would have to do. Then, another idea. He dialed Bill Lord's cell number and waited while it rang and rang and rang, then went to voicemail. Not his lucky day. Last idea. Should have been his first.

Pray. He'd understood from things Connie said that she is a Christian. He knew the Bible was chock-full with references about money. Pulling the leather bound copy from his desk drawer he used the Concordance. Easier, faster in some ways than using the cell phone ap first.

He was flipping the thin pages to the word money. Then, he looked the passages up on his cell's Bible ap. That way he could try different versions. Most of them were to his surprise in the Old Testament. Only one that came up in the New Testament was in 1 Timothy. He tried the different versions on the ap. He had always like the Amplified Bible and pulled that one up.

For the love of money [that is, the greedy desire for it and the willingness to gain it unethically] is a root of all sorts of evil, and some by longing for it have wandered away from the faith and pierced themselves [through and through] with many sorrows. 1 Timothy 6:10

It wasn't exactly what he had hoped for. He didn't believe he, nor Connie, was greedy, nor had she gained it unethically. It was a gift to her. He knew the bank would receive a percentage, a small one, for orchestrating the donation. That is what it was called because the group who gave it to her was a non-profit. He was pondering that when his cell rang.

"Hi, Jaeda! I am so excited. I just talked with

my mom, and for the first time in years she was enthusiastic for me. Actually, blessed me with the Jabez prayer." She sighed so loudly he almost put the phone down. "Now, what's up?"

~

Jaeda pinched his nose again, and this time wiped his brow. It was his mistake, but how could he tell her? Bill Lord hadn't returned his call yet, so he was on his own.

She sat across from him again and stared, her azure eyes wide, still reminding him of the ocean. Why couldn't he escape that vision? He wanted to dive into them, those pools of blue.

"W – well," he stammered. "Seems there is a glitch in our budgeting for your windfall."

"Oh?" She blinked rapidly, and he was sure he saw mist under her eyelids. It would kill him to disappoint her. She was so trusting. How could he rectify this? Be honest, confess. He pinched his nose.

"The mistake was mine. But, not only will I figure it out, but I will correct it." He wiped his brow again. How would he correct it? He didn't have that kind of available cash. Maybe he would lose his job.

~

Connie was shocked. How could this have happened? She would have to give up the new design space. Hard to blame Jaeda because she was there doing the numbers with him. Still, he was the expert. Maybe not. She tried as the Bible taught in 1 Thessalonians to "give thanks in all circumstances" and focus on the overall blessing, the support of the group that funded her. She needed advice. Again.

Logan Lovejoy was delighted to meet with Connie again. She waved to him from the same little round table, but she didn't look happy. A latte was sitting in front of her, and so was a balled up paper napkin. He ordered a venti Americano with an extra shot of espresso. He guessed he would need it. He was right.

"How did this happen, Connie?" His brows rose in question. "I thought you and that banker guy did a budget."

She shrugged. "We did. I thought he was an expert. Guess not." She looked miserable.

Logan turned his paper cup around in his hands several times wishing he had bought a ceramic one for Lydia. Think, man, think. How can you help her? Maybe the banker calculations were not as off as Connie thought.

"Can you get a copy of the budget? I'd like to see it. I should have asked for it before we went real estate shopping. I just trusted how much you said you could spend each month on rental for a studio." He slapped the table, and both cups jumped. "Some realtor I am."

"No, Mr. Lovejoy, not your fault. I'm not good

29

at budgeting, and certainly not at math. But," she continued with a sigh, "I am good at trusting." She stared off into space. "Not so much anymore."

"Still, it sounds like a glitch, an oversight. Maybe made in haste and too much excitement. May I see a copy of it?"

"Of course. I will text Jaeda right now." After sending the message she laid her phone on the table, and it started to vibrate. "Still on silent." She grinned. "I hate that bing sound."

"Me, too, but if I don't have it activated, I sometimes don't hear it. Like over the car engine noise. I do have Bluetooth, but I don't use it much. Unless I'm talking business with a client. I -"

She interrupted him. "Wow! Guess he does feel guilty. He's sending a copy over with a courier." Her eyes were wide, and she finally took a sip of her latte. "Ugh! Cold. Sorry I interrupted you. Guess we should wait for the courier to appear."

He nodded, had the barista refill their cups and said a silent prayer, hoping for the best. Maybe if he looked over the entire budget he could find a solution so she wouldn't have to renege on the studio rental. She had already signed the contract.

Ten minutes later Logan slipped a wad of papers out of the envelope the young man with the unruly hair had handed to Connie. He brought up the calculator on his phone and started punching in numbers. He used the realtors' formula for the percentage of income one should spend on housing. Although Connie's windfall wasn't exactly income, he thought of it that way. Then, it hit him.

"Connie, estimate for me how much you make net each month." His mouth went dry, hoping. He added that number to the windfall number.

"Now, tell me how much you spend on models and seamstresses. What their salaries arc, approximately." She did some finger calculating and explained it varied. He ball-parked it and deducted that as expenses.

"If you had to, absolutely had to, what could you eliminate or cut back on?"

"Well," she hesitated. "Doug wants to send me a new male model." She bit her bottom lip and made a face. "I hate male models! So into themselves. Always scrawny and egotistical, no fun to design for."

"What about if you found one to do it for free, or minimal compensation?"

She rolled her eyes. "Good idea, but who?"

Logan took an audible deep breath. Now he remembered he had seen the man he had in mind once in passing when he was standing in line at the bank. Considering his error in the budget, maybe … "What about Jaeda?"

"What! A buff black model? Mmm." Her expressive face broke into a wide grin, then she giggled. "That could be fun."

CHAPTER FIVE

*J*aeda shook his head hard. No, no, no! What would the bank think? Or, did anyone have to know? He texted Connie. "I will pray on it."

"You pray? You're Christian?" was the text she sent back. "You did say you'd find a way to compensate for the error." She added a smiley face and an emoticon of praying hands.

He asked what it would involve. He obviously couldn't do it during banking hours, couldn't risk his job. Especially, when he was planning to apply for a transfer to Scottsdale.

They decided to meet and discuss. He wanted to see some of her designs, maybe meet the Doreen she'd told him about. The one with the shorter leg who is her model prototype for disability designs. Had she designed for any male clothes? It was important to him to keep his image, not be subjected to attire that smacked of non-gender. He tugged at the knot in his tie. It had to be all male clothes, nothing else.

The next afternoon he stood on a raised round thing while a petite older woman named Alice took his measurements. He was uncomfortable with some of them, but she assured him it was necessary. "How can Miss Connie know what size to tell the seamstress to make?" She glanced up through foggy glasses to admonish him. At this moment, Alice was in charge. "Stay still, mister. Stop wiggling. Inseams are important, especially on men." Yep, she was in charge.

Then came the photographs – dozens it seemed. From every angle, even up. "Miss Connie will use these for inspiration. Especially, if she has trouble remembering what you look like." She giggled. "Doubt that, though."

He put on his real clothes in a flimsy dressing room. Maybe female models didn't mind the curtain that barely closed it off, but he did. When he stepped out, Alice was gone, but another beautiful woman stood beside Connie. Tall. Naturally dark blonde hair swept up.

"Jaeda, this is Doreen, another Candy Cane.

She is one of my models."

Doreen extended her hand and grasped his firmly which made him like her immediately. Other than Connie, few women did that. Most had wimpy milkshake handclasps. Why did they think that was appealing?

~

Doreen turned to Connie. Jaeda had finally left on his unique motorcycle after an obligatory hug to Connie.

"Wow! Where did you find the dude?" Doreen's comment unnerved Connie.

"Bank. Bank officer. Long story."

"So, tell. I have time."

Connie hesitated. "Remember my telling you about the financial backing from the mystery group?"

Doreen nodded. "He a part of it?"

"No, he is an intermediary. But, I had to meet with him to budget the money I was receiving."

"Go on. This sounds intriguing." Doreen locked eyes with Connie. "You sweet on him?"

"Didn't think so," she paused, "until today. He is quite a hunk, huh?"

"You betcha, as my Swedish grandpa used to say. You betcha!"

"Can't go anywhere. Big social problem, right?"

"I don't know. Might be less social and more

family problem. Get my drift?"

Connie did. For once in her twenty seven years Mom had seemed happy for her. She tried to recall the conversation. All she could remember was a mumbled "I am proud of you." That was enough. Now, if she decided, or chose, to date a man of color, how would Mom react? She wasn't sure she had the courage to go there. Then she remembered her friend Marchesa in fifth grade, the first friend of color she had brought home.

So many new people had moved into the neighborhood, and Connie was thrilled to make a new friend. It had upset her that some of the snooty girls ignored Marchesa. Was it because she was new, or because she was African-American? Connie hadn't cared. Mom had greeted both of them with cookies and milk, shook Marchesa's hand, even hugged her hello. Both moms had become friends often chatting together on their phones. No cell phones then, but both worrying about their daughters.

Connie remembered the time she and Marchesa and two other friends were shopping at Ralphs for treats to have after a movie night at her house. The clerk looked at Marchesa and said, "How do you do that? How do you get your hair in all those tiny braids? Does it take hours?"

Connie was appalled and embarrassed for her friend. She wanted to crawl into one of the grocery bags. But, Marchesa looked the insensitive woman in the eye and said, "Yes, it does take hours, but it lasts for weeks." She was so proud of her friend. When they got home she told Mom who shook her head in disgust and hugged Marchesa. Would Mom remember that incident?

~

Jaeda tossed his helmet on the sofa. Usually he stored it in the bike. But, today he was filled with strange uncertainties. He was out of routine. His little dog Jake leaped around his legs begging for attention. How could he refuse? Jake was all he had now that Keona was gone. He still had hopes of moving to Scottsdale. He loved the area and all it offered, and he especially loved that it supported motorcycle events. Maybe he could share that with Connie. Or, maybe he shouldn't.

He fried a steak and put a pre-wrapped sweet potato in the microwave. He depended on easy to prepare food and good old Stouffer's. As often as he ate their entrees maybe he should buy some stock in Nestle the distributor. He cut open the golden potato slicing it down the middle, then loaded it with huge chunks of butter and fresh ground pepper over the two halves. Suddenly, he felt guilty. If he was going to help Connie out by modeling, he had better cut back on the calories. Since Keona left he had been lax, probably trying to silently defy her for all those leafy green dinners. Now, he had a whole new budding career to think about. Or a part-time career, at least.

He was just reaching in the freezer for a Ghirardelli dark chocolate square when his cell buzzed. He really should take the ring tone of a revving motorcycle off. Not very professional. The screen told him it was a call from Connie. What now?

"Hi! You busy?" Her voice trilled over the phone like music.

"Not really. What's up?" He hoped no more fittings to schedule.

"Uh . . ." Silence. Finally, "Wondered if you were free for a cup of coffee."

"Sure. Where?" They arranged to meet at the Corona del Mar Starbucks. But, he wondered … was this a date?

~

She did it. Sort of. She initiated the plans. Now she wasn't sure. Maybe he would think it was a business meeting. Maybe he would think it too forward of her. She put on a light blue low-cut blouse, one of her own favorite designs. The flirty patterned skirt swirled around her legs just above the knees. Adding about ten jangle bracelets and a watch with a blue band that matched the blouse, she felt very feminine. How would he see her?

At the last minute she decided on long, dangly silver earrings that hung below her hairline. They complimented the strappy silver five inch heels with her blue polished toes peeking out. How would he react? She wasn't the uncertain girl who he first met when she sat across from him in the bank. She leaned forward toward the full length mirror. A tiny bit of cleavage showed emphasizing her snowy skin. Although Jaeda wasn't dark black, more cocoa colored, they would be an interesting study in contrasts. If anyone even noticed.

~

Jaeda got there first and grabbed a tiny table out front on the busy sidewalk. He loved the evening air, even with the noise of traffic and the occasional fumes. Maybe all the cycle riding had made him immune. He saw a vision of loveliness in over-sized sunglasses practically skipping up the sidewalk. Who was that doll with the flirty hair and the moist crimson lips? As she got closer, his chest tightened. The low sun illuminated the whiteness of her arms. Very white, pristine. Way out of his league.

"Good evening, Jaeda." She pushed the sunglasses on top of her head and touched his shoulder with a delicate, blue-tipped hand. He looked up from the tabletop where he'd been day-dreaming, and almost tipped over the metal chair when he scooted back to stand.

"Connie?" How stupid was that, Jaeda. Use your wits, or what's left of them. "Y – you look lovely, ravishing." Did he say that right? He didn't want to be too forward, but she honestly did.

"Thank you, Sir." Her face broke into a teasing grin, and she laughed a quick tinkling sound. "Tonight I am not the business woman in the power suit. Tonight I want to relax and have fun."

He nodded. About all he could do. Where was his voice?

"Oh, you wore my fav shirt." She tweaked the collar of the dark red one he'd worn the day they met. "I love that color on you."

He was going to lose it. Where had this metamorphosis come from? "I – I thought you maybe wanted to discuss business. I was wrong?"

She licked her lips, like she'd told him models were instructed to do before a photo. She batted her eyes and displayed that mischievous grin again. "You betcha you were wrong." She laughed softly. "One of Doreen's Swedish grandpa's expressions. You betcha," she repeated and laughed again. She was flirting, with him. And, he liked it. Maybe too much.

"What did you have in mind for fun and relaxing?" He needed to process this and be prepared.

She cocked her head. "Do you like to dance?"

"Love to, but I'm not very good." There, he'd admitted it. He really should look up Arthur Murray. Keona always chastised him at weddings

39

for not even knowing how to waltz.

"Not to worry. I'm not very good, either. But, I love to. Maybe we can lead each other."

"You have a place in mind?" He had lost control of this. Was it a date?

"Sort of. I remember the Balboa Pavilion used to have dance nights. Wonder if it still does. Mmm. Should have checked before inviting you." She raised those expressive eyebrows and clasped his hand. "If not tonight, there is always the bumper cars, the Ferris wheel, even that windy, but romantic boat ride. Come on. Let's do it."

~

Connie's insides were shaking like they'd been put in a blender on high speed. How had she had the nerve to do this? Something had overcome her normal reticence. Had she lost all discernment? She wasn't usually a forward person, not with men anyhow. After a bad college experience, she avoided them. Especially male models. But, she had succumbed to gorgeous Bill Lord Junior and gone out to dinner with him that one time. He had been almost too polite, giving her the message he wasn't all that interested in her. When he started dating Doreen, she knew why.

She slid into the passenger seat of Jaeda's little sports car and prayed silently.

He started to laugh. "This will be a fun evening. Thanks, Connie. I am excited about it."

She gave a wan smile. "Hope so."

He reached across the console and laid his hand on hers. "You sorry you invited me?"

She sighed. No, she wasn't, but would she have the nerve to tell him about her reservations? "No," she finally said. "I like you a lot. But, I've never asked any man on a date before, in all my twenty-seven years."

"Especially a black man, I bet?"

"That has nothing to do with anything. Honest," she said. But, she knew she was lying. It had everything to do with them.

"Connie," he said. "I am so flattered you asked me to join you this evening, but," he hesitated, "we are not the ideal Newport Beach couple. I am sure heads will turn and eyebrows will raise. We may even hear whispered snide remarks." He squeezed her hand. "Can you handle that?" He glanced over at her. "Maybe we should cancel."

"No! Not on your life, or mine," she chuckled. "I have made a grown up decision, and I will stick with it. I like you a lot. You are more than my banker, more than a model, you are my friend. At least I hope so." She looked at him questioningly. Did he believe her?

~

They were in luck. It was Friday evening and the Pavilion was having dance night, for a fee. Jaeda insisted on paying even though he was

41

Connie's guest. Was that what he was? He still had reservations about this non-date, as Connie called it. He loved being with her, being seen with her. Didn't matter her skin color. She was a beautiful, dynamic woman. If only she wasn't exuding so much sex. Besides her lovely attire and her beautiful face and figure, she projected sensuality.

He didn't think it was intentional, as if she was deliberately trying to come on to him. He knew she was a Christian, and when she had explained about the Candy Canes, he knew all the girls had taken a vow of celibacy until marriage. But, he had been married, and whether it was testosterone or hormones or just being male, he desired her.

Jaeda made a special effort to straighten his tie, tuck in his shirt and pull up his pants to sit at the right spot on his waist. He wanted her to be proud of him. Then he thought, why shouldn't she? He was a bank manager for one of the biggest corporations, and now, he was a model. All that had no association to his skin color.

The funky band started to play, and he pulled Connie into his arms. Strong arms. He hoped she realized that. The first tune was a waltz. She smiled up at him, and he let her guide him. Someday, he would learn the simple steps. But, for now, he was just happy to have her in his arms.

He was rewarded with be-bop. Was it still called that? At least it was what he knew and was more comfortable with. He swung her around, thrilled her skirt lifted and twirled like it was flying into the wind. When she leaned toward him, he saw the pristine whiteness of her chest. He was a goner.

~

"That was so fun!" She was panting, trying to catch her breath. "I loved it when you twirled me. I hope you like to dance as much as I do?" She had made it a question and waited for his answer.

"I do. Now. I was never into dancing, but with you I love it." He hoped he had given the right answer because it was the truth. With her he could do anything. Hadn't he proved that standing for hours to be measured on a pedestal by Alice with her cloudy glasses? Surely, he had demonstrated his attraction to her by coming here tonight.

"Why. Don't. You. Take off that tie?" She tugged at the four in hand knot and loosened it. "Seems so restrictive." He got caught up in her melodic laughter and yanked the offending noose off to tuck it into his pocket. He drew her into his arms again just as a blonde woman tapped her on the arm. She was about Connie's age and seemed friendly. So, he released her, assuming Connie would want to chat with an old friend. Connie pulled back.

She said a simple "Hi, nice to see you, Vicki. Excuse us, please."

What was that all about? The other girl

persisted.

"But, aren't you going to introduce me? He is so handsome, and so …" Her words faded off. But, he could guess.

"Okay, but quickly. We are having such a good time." She gestured to Jaeda. "This is my friend, Jaeda. Jaeda, Vicki from high school."

He did the "Nice to meet you," and extended his hand, but Vicki seemed reluctant to take it. She did the fingertip touch, then withdrew and wiped her hand on her clothes. Did she think his skin color would rub off on her?

~

They were back at Starbucks, finally having coffee.

"This isn't going to work, Connie, my Funny Connie." He had started to call her that during one of the more enthusiastic dances when she couldn't stop twirling and spinning. What right did he have to call her "My Funny Connie?" None.

"What isn't?" She tilted her head and seemed to be peering at his eyes. Was she playing dumb?

"Surely, you know what I mean. You and me." Suddenly he felt a foot caressing his leg under the table. She had slipped off a shoe and slid her toes under the hem of his pant leg. "Stop that, Connie, please."

"Why? You embarrassed?" She giggled and tickled his ankle more. "This, may I remind you,

Jaeda, is the twenty-first century. And, it's California, not Arkansas."

He shoved back his chair and towered above her. "Let me walk you to your car." Then, he remembered. "Do I have a fitting tomorrow?"

"Thank you. But, I can walk myself to my car. And, yes, you do. Two p.m." She reached down and slipped her silver sandal back on, stood up to face him and even with the five inch heels only reached his chin. Giving a little bird wave, she said, "See you then."

CHAPTER SIX

"*O*h, Nat, what am I going to do? I am so attracted to him." She waited for Natalie's reply on the other end of the call. But, all she heard was silence broken periodically with a tsk sound. "Nat, you there? I really need advice."

"Aw, Con. This is tricky. More difficult than the Cindy and Rob situation. You did say Jayden is a Christian, right?"

"Yes, and his name is Jaeda." She spelled it. "I know, unusual."

"Very."

"He said his little sister named him. Cute, huh?"

"Uh, yeh. What else do you know about him?"

"I know he's smart, obviously, since he is an officer at the bank. He was born and pretty much brought up in New York; got the West Coast bug. But, not for acting, just business. Has an MBA, dresses real snazzy." She raised her voice a tad. "Very classy guy."

"Well, is color the only problem he has with dating you?"

"I – I think so. That's what he brought up. But, it doesn't bother me at all." Then she remembered. "Do you recall that Vicki shrew in high school. The one who was always making fun of us being a group called the Candy Canes?"

"The one with the rich parents who owned a yacht? If that's the one, yes, I remember her. Super jealous, wanted to be on the swim team but didn't have the strokes down, nor the stamina."

"That's the one. I think her last name was Hamilton. Her dad also owned a yacht brokerage, not just a yacht. Parents got divorced when the mom ran off with the little brother's soccer coach." She started to giggle remembering the neighborhood gossip. Then she remembered the dad, as rich as he was, had a drinking problem. So sad. She shared that with Natalie. "No wonder Vicki is the way she is."

"Why are we talking about her?" Natalie asked.

"Oops, sorry. She was at the Pavilion last night;

insisted on being introduced to Jaeda. Sort of sneered at him. Or, was it me? Or, both of us? Anyway, she managed to spoil the moment."

"I wouldn't let a girl like that even bother you. She was either just curious or jealous. Probably jealous now that word has gotten around you are an almost famous fashion designer."

Connie laughed out loud. "I wish. But sweet of you to say so. You might be part right, though." She smiled to herself. "Maybe you should meet him. Then you would know why I like him so much."

~

Doreen! Connie snapped her fingers. Of course she should call Doreen. She at least had met Jaeda. As she pressed the little symbol on the phone for Doreen's number, she got an idea.

"Hey, Connie, what's up? You need me today?" Doreen was such a wonderful friend, and now employee. Always eager to help.

She wasn't scheduled for a fitting today, but Connie was sure she'd be agreeable to come in. She would pay her, of course, both in salary and clothes. Doreen loved the clothes Connie had designed for her, and Connie allowed her a lot of input about color and fabric and how they felt. For instance, "These pants swish around my ankles too much and get caught up in my orthopedic shoe." Doreen's assessments were very helpful and a big reason Connie's special disability line was gaining acclaim.

Two Orange County publications, one a local magazine and one a newspaper, had written it up with a stunning picture of Doreen on the L.A. runway. The contest to name the line was still going on, so hopefully there would be more publicity and more entries.

Connie shook the cobwebs out of her head and returned to the moment. Doreen's soft voice always touched her. For such a tall, and some would say aptly endowed, woman, Doreen's voice was startlingly melodic. Many people on first meeting her thought it would be deep and booming.

"Yes, it would be great if you have time to come in today. I just got an idea for you and Jaeda. Remember him? You met him the other day."

"Do I ever. But, he doesn't have a disability, does he?"

"Only that he's black." Connie chuckled.

"I guess that makes him different from your other male models, like Junior. Does he ride?"

"Yes, but he rides a different sort of cycle. I'll send you a website link so you can look it up. Junior won't be put out. Jaeda's cycle isn't a Harley. It has a small sidecar for his little dog. Jake I think its name is."

"Is coming in today what you called about?" Doreen asked.

"Not really." Connie paused before going into

'the problem,' as she called it. Jaeda's firm words came back to her – "This won't work."

"That idiot," Doreen exclaimed. "What is he afraid of? His job? His family? And," she continued, "you two just had one date. It's not like you are serious, yet."

Connie imagined Doreen's smile on the other end. "No. Not yet, anyway. But, he doesn't want to even give it a chance."

"We will see. I will be there at two, okay?"

~

Jaeda pulled up on his cycle and scooped Jake out of the sidecar. The little dog needed a change of scenery. He was always well behaved, so when he looked up at Jaeda with those dark brown eyes and wiggled his bottom, he couldn't resist.

"Oh, how adorable!" Doreen ran toward the tiny canine and scooped him up in her arms.

"He is so cute!" Connie exclaimed. "Maybe he can be in an ad."

Jaeda hadn't expected this display of emotion for the Jakester. He was glad the women liked him. With Jaeda's schedule Jake was left alone a lot.
"Glad you all like him." He patted Jake's head, told the dog to sit. He did and wiggled in place.

Connie got down to business. She had Jaeda and Doreen stand together on the platform. "Hold hands, please. And look at each other adoringly. I need to get this image in my mind."

"What about the dog?" Doreen asked. "He is so super cute."

"Good idea, Doreen. Jaeda, pick up pup and cuddle him under your arm."

Jake was thrilled to be held, but he had trouble being still. After a few treats that Jaeda had in his pocket, he settled down. "Maybe," Jaeda laughed, "you should give your models treats, too."

Connie smirked at him and put on a fake smile. "Maybe I will."

She couldn't remember a model situation going so well. Even the little dog posed and seemed happy. That gave her a crazy idea, or was it crazy?

CHAPTER SEVEN

"What? You want Jake to model?" Jaeda held the phone out in front of him to stare at it. Was she serious? A dog model?

"Yep. Fun idea. I will design matching outfits for you both. Super cute, and people suck up dog attire." Jaeda held his breath, then spewed out a whoosh. The idea made him feel silly, foolish even. "I – I'm not sure, Connie. Seems a bit off the wall. You serious?" he asked, hoping she was kidding.

"Absolutely. It will be a great promotion for my line." She must have heard his silence. "What's wrong? You no like?"

"Not sure. Seems over the top to me." He

thought about how his bank colleagues might see the ads, him in the same fashion attire as his little dog. Ugh. Embarrassing. Few of them even knew he had a dog, especially a diminutive one. Nor a modeling career. This could ruin his real career.

~

Connie stewed. What was wrong with Jaeda? She thought he'd be pleased little Jake would be part of the new line. Guess it was the old macho thing. Unless ... the dog was a big, drooling rescue dog, or close. She called Doreen.

"I think it's a great idea. Maybe he has some ego issues?" She made it a question, probably hoping Connie might know.

"I never thought about that, but maybe." She tried to gather her thoughts. "He is a big man, stature wise. Maybe that is an issue for him. I thought him confident, not into worrying about petty opinions." She asked another question of Doreen. "You think his color might have something to do with it?"

"Can't say, but never would have thought about that after meeting him."

"He seems reticent. I don't want to put him in an uncomfortable position, but I love the idea of the male and dog model combo. And," she continued, "he is doing this to make up for his budget mistakes."

"I have an idea," Doreen said. "Remember

Candy's mom's dog, Striker?"

"Sort of. What?"

"He is a big, lumbering dog. Maybe I could have him as my dog. That way it wouldn't be just a tiny dog, but two that would appeal to more audiences."

"Does Striker know you? Would he be comfortable with you? And, you with him?"

"That dog would be comfy with anyone who gives him a treat. He would sit at my heals salivating." Doreen laughed. "He has a sweet face, too. I think it would be worth a try."

~

Connie got all excited about the dog idea. What would make it even more fun was Doreen, tall and slender, but very feminine, with Striker; and tall, masculine, buff Jaeda with tiny Jake. That and the two skin colors. This could be a breakthrough for her design business.

She started sketching, then she called her seamstress and photographer. She went online to explore fabrics, but even with her merchant number they would take too long to arrive. She wanted the fabrics yesterday. She jumped in her car and pulled up next to Fabric Depot. If she could find the perfect fabrics that she could order quantities of online? That was the question. She clasped her hands in front of the steering wheel and prayed. Surely, God had given her this idea.

She dragged several bolts of fabrics from her car and set them up near her drafting table for inspiration. She had been assured she could order them online in quantity, and reorder them on her merchant account. To make sure, she got it in writing.

She went to work doing what she did best. It was two a.m. when she flipped over a blank page on her sketching pad. She was satisfied, she had done her best, God's inspirations.

Doreen came for a pre-fitting Monday afternoon. She had borrowed Striker who lumbered next to her, and, unfortunately, slobbered. He was a sweet dog, loved the attention and sat still when asked. Connie thought how adorable he would look in plaid.

"I don't want to diss your ideas, but don't you think plaid is not right for a big dog?" Doreen said. "Seems like little Jake would look cute in plaid. How about camo for Striker? Or, stripes?"

"Plaid is all the rage this season," Connie said. "What about tiny plaid for Jake and bigger for Striker? And big plaid for Jaeda and small for you?"

Doreen thought about it, then said, "Try it. You have sketches?"

Connie brought them out, and before any fabric was cut donned Doreen and Striker in shawl-like drapes for effect. Jaeda finally showed up with Jake. Both seemed to grimace at being subjected to this somewhat embarrassing situation. He tucked the little dog under his right arm and turned toward Doreen.

"Hey, man, smile," she said. "This is the fun part when we can give input and our opinion about the fabs."

"The fabs?"

"Fabrics, how they look, colors, our ideas to the designer."

"We get to do that?" He sounded confused.

"Yes. Connie is all open to ideas, and," she said, "opinions. Our opinions matter since we will be wearing her designs in ads and on the runway."

"What? In ads? Runway? Online, too?"

"Yes, print ads, and yes online. Sometimes YouTube." Doreen looked at him head on. "You have a problem with that?"

"Not sure. Sort of took me by surprise." He looked at Connie. "This part of the deal?"

"Yes, Jaeda, but you can opt out of it. You decide."

"Maybe I will." He sounded very firm.

~

They had fun with the plaid ideas and found themselves in fits of laughter, especially about the dogs in the design. All at once Connie raised her arms and shouted, "Yes! Got it."

Jaeda and Doreen looked at her with puzzled expressions.

"We won't overdo the plaid. In fact, too much plaid is distracting to the eye. Little Jake," she rubbed the tiny dog's ear, "will have a plain doggy vest with a plaid collar. Jaeda will sport a plaid tie matching the design in Jake's collar, and … maybe plaid pants." She tilted her head and scratched her ear. "Hmm. Might be too much, make Jacda look like a wannabe dandy." She laughed at her own mental illustration.

"Whew!" Jaeda blew out a breath. "And, by the way, Connie, black guys don't wear plaid." His hearty laugh boomed through the room. He apparently couldn't resist more humor, so with a stone face, he leaned forward nearly slipping off the pedestal. "But," he said in a flat, controlled voice, "they do swim."

Doreen couldn't contain herself and she, too, almost toppled off the pedestal she was laughing so hard. "Hey, Con, we could make him an honorary member of the Candy Canes." By this time all three of them were holding their sides, and the two startled dogs both woofed. What was even funnier was little Jake's penetrating bark was almost louder than big Striker's.

"Oh, my gosh!" Connie was swallowing her laughter and ended up hiccupping, noisily. That set them all off again. Finally, after turning her back and holding her nose, she found control. "Back to work, gang. I can't afford to pay for hilarity breaks.

But, it was fun." She stepped back and surveyed Jaeda's tall form. "No, you don't have a plaid physique. You're too conservative to dress like a groovy guy." He stuck his tongue out at her.

"I like the idea of a plaid tie, Con," Doreen said. "But, what about a linen blazer with plaid elbow patches? Or, would that be too much?"

"Hey, I have a pair of plaid high tops in my collection. That might be the finishing touch," Jaeda said.

"What do you mean 'collection'?" Connie asked. Both women stared at him.

"Oh, when I was on the team in high school and then college, I started collecting shoes. Some are copies of famous basketball greats, like Michael Jordan, and some are just cool ones I fell for and couldn't resist."

"You played basketball? Makes sense. How big is your collection?" Connie was curious.

"About two hundred and fifty."

Doreen gaped at him, and Connie whistled. "I can't believe it. How big is your closet?"

"Bigger now that it's just Jake and me," he said with a grin. "Actually, I do have a pair of plaid laces. More subtle than the shoes. Or," he went on with his brow furrowed, "you could roll my pants up, and I could wear plaid socks." He was laughing, but Connie wasn't.

"Don't tell me," she said, "you have a plaid

cycle helmet, too."

"No, but I do sometimes wear a plaid shirt when I ride."

"And, you said you don't like plaid." She was mocking him, and he knew it, but played along.

"I have an idea, too." Jaeda raised his dark eyebrows as if asking permission to share.
"Go for it." Connie grinned.

"I like the little jacket idea on Jake with a plaid collar. I assume a turned down collar on the jacket? Sort of like a shirt collar?" he asked. Connie nodded.

He leaned down and patted Striker on his broad head. "Amazing dog, but too big for a cutesy collar on a jacket. Actually, too big for a jacket. Clothes are for tiny dogs – shiatzus and min-pins and doxies. How about a wide dog collar and leash in plaid?"

Connie clapped her hands. "I love it! Now, for Doreen."

"How about a floor length plaid pleated skirt?" Doreen said. "No, you wouldn't be able to see Striker's leash. It would blend." Then she snapped her fingers. "A plaid sarong with fringe, and the long part would hide my orthopedic shoe, but the other side would be open almost to the waist. That's the side Striker would be on." She waited for Connie to visualize and nod.

"You and Jaeda would have to change places

since it's your left foot we want to hide, and he would have to hold Jake in his left arm." She closed her eyes and spoke. "You have beautiful legs, Dor, especially the right one. Oops. Hope I didn't offend you." She looked concerned.

"Nope, very realistic about the whole leg thing."

"Maybe a scarf at the neck, or a cute floppy straw hat with a plaid band?" Connie was still thinking.

"I love the hat idea, especially since summer is approaching. You could even put a plaid clip-on bow on my one sandal."

Connie grinned, spun around and clapped her hands together. Jaeda and Doreen got the picture – she was happy.

~

She stayed up half the night sketching, and when they all arrived Tuesday afternoon late, because of Jaeda's bank job hours, she popped a bottle of fizzy apple cider. She whipped out sketches and laid them on the big cutting table. Handing each a plastic glass she said, "We celebrate!"

The two models pointed to the elaborate sketches and made a few suggestions, but nothing Connie couldn't live with. They were both creative and had a grasp of style. The new plaid line would soon be a reality. Alice came in and made a few suggestions, too, based on cut and the woof and warp of the fabrics. "You sure you can order these fabs in quantity?" she asked.

"Got a signed release from the fabric place. My merchant number will work online. Just tell me, after you measure these two, how much you think I should order. I want to keep the designs exclusive enough for only twelve outfits each. Obviously, in varying sizes."

"Will do," Alice nodded. Connie had faith in her. The woman was amazing at calculating sizes and fabric amounts. Maybe she should have helped with the windfall budget process.

~

It was time. She must confront Jaeda soon about his relationship reservations. The more she was around him, especially the last few days for the fittings, the more she was attracted to him.

His physical attributes made her knees weak when she looked at him, especially on the designing pedestal. She remembered being close to him during the waltz at the Balboa Pavilion. She had nestled her nose in his neck and wanted to bury it there. She couldn't get it out of her mind. He had smelled so good she had almost asked him for the name of his cologne, but didn't want to break the spell of the moment. The fast dancing with the spinning and Jaeda swinging her was exhilarating, leaving her breathless. But, that Vicki girl had almost spoiled it.

Connie was determined she wouldn't let her. After she flung the imaginary snake off her arm like Moses had and stomped on it, she felt relieved. And guilty. Vicki was a sad case. Needed prayer. So, Connie sat down on her sofa and prayed for her.

~

First she called Doreen, then Natalie. Both reassured her she did the right and godly thing praying for Vicki.

"Buff up, girl," Doreen said. "You have to examine your heart. Yours, not anyone else's."

"You can't let her determine your relationship with Jaeda," Natalie said with conviction. "Only God can do that."

She still hadn't shared the dating across races thing with the other Candy Canes. Was it because she feared they would discourage it?

"Noelle answered in the middle of fixing dinner. Can I call you back?"

She refused to bother Candy on her second honeymoon, so she emailed Cindy in Costa Rica. It was much easier to explain in an email post.

Finally, she dialed Melanie's number. Surely, God had led her there.

CHAPTER EIGHT

*C*onnie was shocked to hear Melanie's story. She had known about the baby that Melanie had refused to abort, but had a miscarriage instead. Stress the doctors had said. But, Melanie had never shared what the stress was.

"He was black. From the South, very traditional southern African-American. Into black liberation, sort of like the Black Lives Matter movement is today, but not quite as organized. Wanted nothing to do with me except my body." She sighed, and Connie was sure her eyes were filled with tears.

Connie wept with her. That's what Candy Cane sisters did. Then she asked. "How did you meet him? What was the reason and the attraction?"

"I was a college sophomore. I believed in supporting liberation to right the wrongs in racial tensions. We met at a rally, then later joined a sit-in." Melanie sighed loudly and continued. "He was so sincere, and so gorgeous. I had never met anyone like him. Tall, muscular, handsome. But, black. He had a way of touching me, not sexually, just lovingly. But," she finally said, "it was all a sham. Found out later he just wanted to bed a lily white woman. Like a notch on his belt."

Connie hung up the phone after praying with Melanie and thanking her for her candor. What a mess relationships could be. Even those, she thought, between ethnicities like Irish and Italian. Her background was English, French and Swedish, so she'd been led to believe. Still, white and black was more challenging.

She called Jaeda.

~

Jaeda wasn't sure he wanted to pick up his phone. The caller display said Connie. Was he ready to talk with her? He bit his lip, said a short prayer and answered.

"We need to talk," they both said in unison. Then, they laughed.

They decided to meet at good old Starbucks. Thank goodness they had that option.

Connie arrived first, attired in of all things,

plaid. Even though she looked adorable, Jaeda laughed.

"Couldn't resist," she said, laughing, too. "You up for a walk? Maybe on the beach?"

He nodded loving the idea. More private. "But, what about your shoes?" he asked looking down to the delicate silver sandals.

"No problemo. What about yours?"

"One reason I wear athletic shoes. Easy to remove. Let's put both of ours in my car. I was so lucky to get a space on PCH near the coffee shop."

They both reached for each other's hands. After running barefoot a few blocks on PCH, they traipsed down Poppy to Little Corona Beach. The trail from the street to the small inlet beach was tricky, very steep and hard to navigate in bare feet. And there was that big crack in the sidewalk on Poppy that had been there for years. What had they been thinking?

The beach was environmentally protected so no one could, or should, pick up and take any shells or other sea things that had drifted in. Connie was tempted by a starfish, but she loved the ocean and all that God had designed, so she put the tiny invertebrate back on the sand. Then, she turned to Jaeda.

"What?" he asked.

She didn't respond. What did he mean by 'what?' Was the man clueless, or was he bluffing?

Maybe she should give up on him and her dreams of him.

Finally, he pulled her into his arms. She looked up at his adorable face and melted. Then, he spoke.

"This is not right, Connie. Not right. Difficult, challenging. Not right."

She snuggled into his chest. What was not right? If they cared about each other, even hopefully loved each other, how could that be not right in God's eyes?

"Jaeda, do you remember the story in Genesis?" He nodded.

"Do you remember God saying anything about the color of Adam and Eve's skin?"

He shook his head.

"Do you think He divided us, separated us, by skin color?"

"No. But I do believe he made us different for a reason."

~

Connie struggled with the sheets. Nothing had been solved or resolved during the beach walk with Jaeda. She flipped her pillow over twice and finally succumbed to sleep saying the Lord's Prayer. When she awoke at five a.m. she felt much better. God was in control. He had to be, because she wasn't.

~

Jaeda tossed and turned, mentally tapping a rhythm in his brain, what drummers did to relax. He adored Connie, but didn't want to subject her to all the possibilities of hate and publicity of inter- racial relationships. Maybe marriages. That was too much to expect of her. He thought of his family.

He sat up in bed and dialed his little sister's number. They hadn't spoken, actually spoken, in a year. Must have been during Christmas when he flew back to New York. It didn't compute. He hardly remembered, that's how hazy it was. No one had connected, no one had laughed or hugged much, except obligatory. He had lost his family.

CHAPTER NINE

"*I* need family. Are you willing?"

Connie looked at the text from Jaeda again. She was puzzled, and concerned. What did he mean? Was he depressed? "You all right? What was the text about me being family?" She waited for his text to return. When it didn't after fifteen minutes, she texted again. Where was he?

She decided to call him. Voice on voice can make a huge difference.

~

"Sorry," she said in her most empathetic voice. "I couldn't wait. What is wrong?"

She heard rhythmical tapping on the other end.

Finally, after what seemed like a mini-eternity, he cleared his throat.

"First worried, now devastated." She heard a long sigh, maybe a sob? Then the word, "E-Ma, Grandma."

"What?"

"What, Jaeda, tell, share." She sounded like a parrot.

"The question is 'when'?" Now she heard the sob. She thought about all the reasons a grown man would sob, especially after referring to his grandma. Something must be wrong with her.

"Died."

Oh, put a whole different spin on things. She remembered Jaeda was close to his grandmother, but she wasn't sure how to react to this information. From what he had told her the woman was ancient. She hadn't had much experience in the grandparent section of her life. Mom's parents were a lot like her – judgmental, not forthcoming except for Bible verses. Yes, cold.

Daddy's lived so far away she hardly saw them, even when growing up. They were afraid to fly, and driving thousands of miles was out of the question. Yet, the little communication she'd had with them was kind and loving. She remembered Grandma Winfield always sent birthday cards to her with tender thoughts. "I love you, Connie. You are a part of my heart."

She still had those in the box in her closet. Did Sandra have them, too?

She shook herself back to the moment and Jaeda. Trying to understand, she gripped her emotions and modulated her response. If she truly loved this man, she needed to understand his pain and live his life.

"Explain, please." She didn't want to sound unsympathetic or uncaring, but she needed to know.

"She died last night. In her sleep." He paused again, and Connie waited. "A blessing, I guess."
"So sorry, Jaeda. So sorry. I know you loved her very much, and she was a huge part of your life." She waited for a response. What she got was a shock.

"Go with me, please," he begged.
Connie almost put the phone down. What was he asking?

"What are you asking?"

"I want you to go with me, for support. To her funeral."

"Oh, really?" She was reluctant to voice her next question, but she did anyway. "Do they know about us? As a couple?" She wondered if they were 'a couple.' But, at this time it was a moot point, especially in his grief.

"Sort of. I told E-ma, and I mentioned you to Mom. Will you go?"

"Aw, don't know if I should, if it's right." This

time she set the phone on the kitchen counter and pushed the speaker button. She needed coffee, lots of it.

~

Jaeda gently nudged her ahead in the long airport security line. She pulled out her driver license and her ticket. She couldn't believe she was going to New York. For a funeral. Not the city, but in a small town with fields and pastures. At least that's the way he had described it. Cows! Woods! Had she brought the right clothes?

"Did I bring the right clothes?" She turned to him just as the TSA security woman asked her to step forward. The question would have to wait. So would the answer.

They settled into their seats, cramped as expected, but near the front of the plane and next to each other; hers on the aisle so she could get up easily to use the bathroom. Connie shoved her large purse under the seat in front of her, crossed her legs and picked up the airline magazine. What was she expecting? A nirvana moment in an article to calm her and give her direction?

"You okay?"

She was startled by his question. "Of course. Fine." But, she wasn't. She was scared. What would all those people think of her, of Jaeda bringing her to a very special memorial and funeral for a beloved African-American woman? She was determined to be seen as a Christian woman who loved the Lord. Also, as a dear friend of Jaeda's. Was that what she was? At least that was true. She would suck it up, as Candy used to remind her to do.

~

They were greeted at luggage claim by a tall, maybe taller than Jaeda, but blacker than Jaeda, man with a huge smile. Connie liked him immediately.

"Good to meet you, Sister," he said grinning. "Jaeda shared." He grinned again. Just as she wondered who the man was, and why hadn't Jaeda introduced them, he explained.

"I'm Sean, brother-in-law. Sissy's husband." He extended his hand and whooped. "You're okay, girl. Got a nice firm handshake."

Connie was pleased to be so easily accepted. She was taken in by Sean, and his acceptance of her meant a lot. A lot more that she would come to know.

~

The house was old and framed in white over sea green blue overlapping panels. Coming from California, she loved it. Although the porch, called veranda here, was not wraparound, it was wide and welcoming. She had read about homes like this, but had never seen one in person. The flowers bordering the walk she couldn't recognize, but were abundant. Obviously cared for.

She clung to Jaeda's arm. For protection, or to let others know she was special to him? She clasped the brown fabric of his linen sport coat hard until it balled up in her hand. He looked at her funny. "Sorry. Guess I'm a little nervous."

"I understand. If I were meeting your parents, I would be, too," he said smiling down at her from his tallness. "Try to remember who else is with us."

"What do you mean?" She felt dense not understanding his comment.

"God."

"Oh."

She relaxed her grip and stood tall, as tall as her short height allowed. Jaeda was right. God had directed her here, to be with him and support him, so she should buckle down.

The first person to approach her was a tall dark man, taller than Jaeda, or even Sean, if that were possible. He held out both hands to clasp hers and squeezed them affectionately.

"Dad!" Jaeda said and hugged the older man giving kisses on both sides of his face. Next was a diminutive woman in a swirling, colorful dress. One Connie would have loved to have designed. She found herself being hugged warmly.

After Jaeda's mom excused herself, he turned to her. "You okay now?"

"Yes, fine. Very fine."

~

The food was exceptional, and mostly Southern. She hadn't expected that since they were in New York. But, she was hungry and loaded her plate.

"Good appetite!" Jaeda chided her with an earsplitting grin.

She nodded and grinned back with a mouthful of pork slathered in sauce. "E-ma's favorite foods?" she asked.

"Some, but others from neighbors and church people. They are all delicious, right? But, you can tell the difference between Southern and local?"

She nodded, but she wasn't sure.

She set her plate down when the music started. Jaeda whispered in her ear that the piano player was his sister, Valencia.

"Did you take lessons?" she whispered back.

"Tried, but percussion was my passion." He looked at her in a funny way. "No one, not even my dad, understood how I longed to drum. I was the odd guy out. But, in the end, he supported me and paid for drum lessons, and bought me a set of drums for my twelfth birthday." He squeezed her hand, and said, "Shh. Val is playing E-ma's favorite song."

Connie recognized the praise song from church. "I believe in God the Father …" It went on to claim belief in Jesus and the Holy Spirit and that the three were one. It was a favorite of hers, too. One she often found herself humming in the shower. The next song almost broke her heart, and Jaeda squeezed her hands so tight she thought he would crush her fingers. She listened to the almost haunting words and knew they were perfect for E-Ma. The words would ring in her ears and her heart for a long time. Tonight in the hotel she would repeat the words as she tried to fall asleep.

She believed E-Ma's chains were gone and her debt paid, and that the sweet lady would be blessed to see Jesus.

When all the guests, close to a hundred, were crowded tightly into the living room clapped and some started dancing, she relaxed. Just like a church service at home in California. Praising the Lord released so much pent up energy and wonder and awe for Him. Now, if He would only release hers.

~

Connie snuggled under the down comforter in the hotel bed. So many questions invaded her mind. She knew in her heart she was on the brink of falling in love with Jaeda. She thought about several couples she knew, some in church, who were yoked and blessed with diverse racial marriages. One, the wife, was the sister of her pastor's wife, a lily white blonde. The husband was blacker than black, but an adorable man who obviously loved the Lord. His mother was in Connie's Bible study. So, what was her problem?

Finally, she succumbed to sleep humming the praise song. Her phone rang and the alarm chimed at the same time.

~

Today was the memorial service. It seemed bass-akwards as her Nana used to say. Connie laughed remembering Nana's cussword quips turned into fun comments. Nana's Bible was laid on her knees every morning, but she was so down to earth in her life.

Connie dressed for the service. She had worn all black the day before because she wasn't sure what the attire should be. Today she would wear one of her more flamboyant designs. What the heck, E-Ma was being celebrated.

"You up and ready?" Jaeda sounded stressed.

"Almost. Down in five. You okay?" She worried about the tremor in his voice. This had to be huge for him. He had shared some about his love for his E-Ma, how he had spent many summers with her on Coney Island. "We would go to the pier, eat hotdogs, drink orange soda and talk about life."

She would never admit it to him, but she was jealous.

~

She was one of about ten people, almost all women except for a short man, who was white. It felt as if her skin glowed and shined under the dim lights of the community center in the church. She kept rubbing her cheeks. Maybe she should have used one of those tanning products. At least her skin would have looked darker.

Several women reached for her hands and embraced her. They were warm and inviting and accepting. Finally, she felt comfortable, then Jaeda disappeared.

She settled into a seat near the door and plunked her purse on the one next to save for Jaeda. She scanned the printed program and noticed his name was listed after his dad's. Was he up to this? She decided to get a cup of coffee from the side table where drinks were offered. Maybe that would calm her spirit. She was pouring the brew into her plastic cup when she heard two people talking.

"Who does she think she is? E-Ma would be turning over in her grave if she knew he was dating a whitey."

"She is a big California fashion designer. Nothing wrong with that," the other man said.

Connie had to laugh at the comment about her being a 'big California fashion designer.' She wished. But, it hurt her heart to hear the other comment. She carefully looked around hoping to see who had spoken, and so boldly. Everyone had moved away from the drink table. She was standing alone. She recalled a plaid tie she had noticed out of the corner of her eye.

Maybe because she, Doreen and Jaeda had

recently focused on plaid for the new designs. It had caught her attention in her peripheral vision.

Jaeda gripped her arm, lightly, to guide her toward the front of the seating. Somehow it seemed formal. She had expected this gathering to be more spontaneous. Now it seemed rehearsed. She never got to see what E-Ma looked like because the casket was closed. That was fine with her.

From Jaeda's description and the framed photos propped on the baby grand last night, E-Ma was a tiny spit of a thing with tightly braided hair wound around her head and secured with a large, glittering comb. She wasn't sure how old that particular photo was, but guessing from Jaeda's teary comments, the diminutive woman hadn't changed much over the years, nor had the comb. She was seated in the second row next to Jaeda when he squeezed her hand and rose suddenly.

He adjusted his jacket - typical Jaeda always wanting to look spiff and in control. Then, he did the most out of character thing. He took off the jacket and tossed it to Connie. Thankfully, in her surprise she caught it.

She heard muffled whispers behind her. His mother, father and Sissy? She hoped they didn't think his gesture, nor hers, was rehearsed. Loosening his tie he stepped toward the microphone and gave a Jaeda grin. Almost as if he was going to share a secret.

"E-Ma was the most special person in my life." He paused to look at his parents. "Even more special than my wonderful parents." He put the tips of his fingers on his right hand to his lips, made a kissing gesture and flung it toward his parents. Wow, Mr. Dramatic! Connie had never seen this side of him, but she immediately started transferring the thought to Jaeda modeling on the runway in the future. Was that bad of her?

He told about how E-Ma had introduced him to public transportation to go to Coney Island when he was ten; how she insisted he eat a renowned Coney Island hot dog even though he shied away from hot dogs; how it became his favorite food for lunch even as a grown up.

Mostly, though, she had laid on a blanket for long hours with him on the beach watching the people and the waves, and talked. No, he corrected himself, she had listened. For years she had listened to his dreams and hopes and quoted Bible verses. Her love is what got him through high school as an average student. Her love in the monthly letters she wrote to him in a scrawling hand is what inspired him in college. E-Ma didn't understand what an MBA was, but she knew it was important. She still sent letters of encouragement. Even to his California address when he was studying at the University of California at Irvine.

How he had wished she could have been there

to see him receive it, but she was afraid to travel in any way shape or form, except city bus. But, with his parents' help she had sent flowers. A bit embarrassing for a guy, but special nevertheless.

He ended his soliloquy turning to the tiny coffin, leaning over it and kissing it. "I love you, E-Ma, always and forever. Thank you for being you."

~

Connie was glad to be home. Hours and hours on an airplane were not her cup of tea. And, to boot, the free tea the airline served was awful. She even asked the surly flight attendant if she paid extra could she have a premium, special tea? "You must not fly often, dear," the overly made up woman said. That put her in her place. How she would love to have the contract to redesign the airline's uniforms. She tucked that thought into her already over-tucked brain. Maybe, someday.

She was glad she went with Jaeda, but still wasn't sure how much it helped him cope. He seemed comfortable with his family, and he did a spectacular job honoring E-Ma at the celebration of her life. Maybe, she concluded, it was about her color. Her lily whiteness. Tomorrow at the fitting she would ask. But, she never had the chance.

CHAPTER TEN

"*I* feel stupid in plaid," Jaeda tugged at his tie.

Alice was pinning the inseam of Jaeda's trousers when he voiced his opinion loudly. "Ouch, woman, watch where your hands go." Alice had a mouthful of straight pins she spit out at his feet. She turned her salt and pepper head toward Connie and shrugged her shoulders in question. Doreen noticed tears in her eyes.

"Get a grip, mister," Doreen said. "This isn't fun for any of us, but necessary. Your duds have to fit perfectly for print ads and the runway. And YouTube," she added. "You owe Miss Alice an apology," she said with a firm tone and looking him in the face.

"What? The runway?" He glanced over Alice to Connie. "Do I have to do that?"

"Yep, part of the deal."

"No, I can't. It could jeopardize my job. No, can't," he repeated.

Doreen glared at him. "The apology?"

"Oh, yeah, sorry Alice. I was caught off guard. Do what you have to do, but be delicate, please." She nodded, scraped up the pins and took her time sticking them in the pin cushion on her wrist. Connie noticed her glasses seemed more fogged than usual.

~

After Jaeda left with little Jake tucked under his arm, Doreen pulled Connie aside. She had slipped out of her plaid skirt and put on her own clothes, her favorite sweats. She tossed a treat to Striker who laid down with his chin on his forepaws and sighed.

"I'm worried, Con, about the Jaeda guy. How did it go in New York?"

"It went really well, Dor, considering. He was wonderful and attentive and gave a great eulogy for his grandma, and didn't seem a bit embarrassed by me."

"Why would he have been embarrassed? You are the perfect lady, always gracious." She cocked her head exploring Connie's face for the answer.

Connie rolled her eyes.

"Oh, I get it," Doreen said.

"Yep, my whiteness."

"Did that really matter? Did either of you get any negative feedback?"

"Not blatantly. A bit subtly. Thinly veiled." Connie crossed her arms in front of her and rubbed her elbows with her hands. She explained about the nasty remark she heard the one man say, how it had hurt her.

"Con," Doreen placed her hands on her friend's shoulders not too gently. "If you really care about Jaeda, and," she paused to be sure Connie was paying attention, "if you have any kind of a future together, that remark was just the appetizer. More to come, maybe for a lifetime."

Connie nodded and collapsed in Doreen's arms weeping. "It's so confusing. I really like him, but not just as a friend." She searched Doreen's face, then confessed. "I think I'm falling in love with him. I feel so lost." Doreen smiled and hugged her.

~

Jaeda kicked the sheets off his feet and Jake growled. Jaeda growled back, but more to the empty room than to Jake who had settled down again taking over more space on the bed. What was he going to do? "Please, God, guide me," he pleaded whispering out loud. His whispered words seemed to bounce around the room, and he kicked at the sheets again. He wasn't sure what was disturbing him more, his family's overly gracious acceptance of Connie or the stupid runway walk in his future. It was a senseless comparison, and he knew it. Both were ego-centered, both silly worries that could be overcome with God's grace.

Then it hit him. In bed, in the middle of the night. It was Connie. His feelings for her. He got out of bed and sat on the lone chair in his room, the one Keona had insisted on buying to sit on to put on her shoes. Silly, he'd thought at the time. Now, he was glad to have another spot to pray and concentrate besides the edge of the bed. He settled into the elaborate brocade fabric and wondered why he hadn't ditched this chair and replaced it with a more masculine one. Another thought for another time. He shook his head, maybe to dislodge the cobwebs, and opened his Bible, the print one instead of the cell phone app one.

He wasn't sure why his fingers went to James. He had hoped for some insight from Proverbs, or maybe John, but James it was. James 5:9 told him to not grumble against other believers. Mmm. A message about Alice and Doreen, and even Connie?

His fingers flipped a few pages back to land on James 1. He had asked God to guide him, so? He was not asking in the right way, but in a double-minded way. The **Epistle writer** confirmed it. He read the passages again. Was his faith being tested? He wanted the 'crown of life' that was promised to him. He wanted to 'be mature' without finding fault. He wanted the 'pure joy.' He wanted Connie's love. He read the passage again, out loud this time. Loudly.

2 Consider it pure joy, my brothers and sisters, whenever you face trials of many kinds, 3 because you know that the testing of your faith produces perseverance. 4 Let perseverance finish its work so that you may be mature and complete, not lacking anything. 5 If any of you lacks wisdom, you should ask God, who gives generously to all without finding fault, and it will be given to you. 6 But when you ask, you must believe and not doubt, because the one who doubts is like a wave of the sea, blown and tossed by the wind. 7 That person should not expect to receive anything from the Lord. 8 Such a person is double-minded and unstable in all they do. . . .

He skipped a few verses hoping the one he clung to was the right one. For him.

12 Blessed is the one who perseveres under trial because, having stood the test, that person will receive the crown of life that the Lord has promised to those who love him.

Jaeda closed the book and crawled into bed. Jake woofed in his sleep.

10 CHAPTER NAME

CHAPTER ELEVEN

*C*onnie shuffled in her fuzzy slippers to the bathroom. She turned on the shower and stepped in to almost scalding water. The spray felt awesome on her aching back. Bending over with Alice yesterday while she was pinning Jaeda and Doreen had taken its toll. She needed to work out again, but time was still of the essence. Maybe it was those staying up until two a.m. nights. Hard to rise at six to run to the gym.

Doreen had given her the speeches. The Biblical and Candy Cane speeches. Where was her faith? She felt as if she had lost it and was wandering. After she dressed she called Natalie and hoped.

She could hear Natalie shuffling papers. Probably at her desk in her gym office. She apologized for interrupting. "Hey, girl, that's what Candy Canes are for – prayer." Nat's voice gave her courage and confirmation.

She shared everything with Natalie; the trip to New York, the incident with the negative comment, the love displayed to her by Jaeda's family, the silly tea request on the airplane, even Jaeda's runway reluctance. Everything.

Suddenly realizing she would be late for church, even the ten o'clock service, she thanked Natalie with a blessing and hung up.

That's when her cell rang. Jaeda.

~

Jaeda could hardly believe he had boldly asked to go to church with her. And, that she told him to wear nice jeans or very casual clothes. His mother would disinherit him if she knew. His father would ask what kind of church it was. Connie had giggled in delight at his request, so he was committed and pulled into a First Time Visitor parking spot – next to Connie.

"Hey, you aren't a first timer! You sure you should be here?"

"I know," she said, "but so few use these spots,

and when I'm running late I do because they are right in front."

He noticed there were about five more empty spots, and no cars pulling into them. The praise music was booming into the large quad. Mariners was a huge church, enormous by his standards. They walked down a double set of stairs from the parking lot before even getting close to the sanctuary. She reminded him it is called a worship center or auditorium.

When they finally entered, he understood why. Must be many hundreds of bodies in many layers. They climbed more stairs to the second large tier where Connie found two seats in a middle row, so they had to scoot past a dozen people. Whew! She explained she liked to sit up high so she could see the whole stage. No complaining from him. He was the guest.

The worship team was led by guitarist Tim Timmons. He had heard his songs on the radio and felt at least he knew someone there. He especially liked the ones Tim had written himself. Learning he could buy a CD after service at the bookstore, he knew he would head over there. If Connie agreed.

How, he wondered, could anyone fellowship with other believers in such an enormous crowd? As people poured out after hearing and watching Pastor Kenton race across the stage while delivering a dynamic message and a thousand voices singing the last praise song, he found out. He and Connie had gotten separated when she went to the ladies room. Looking around for her in the quad, he discovered her chatting and hugging a group of worshipers. Not all women as he would have expected. About half men, and a few children. Finally, she excused herself, waved and trotted over to him. Clasping his arm she guided him to the crowded bookstore. What a treat!

He browsed as quickly as possible in several sections and ended choosing two of the latest Tim Timmons CDs. When he got to the counter to pay, after standing in a long, snaking line, and having déjà vu of the TSA lines at the airports, he saw the point of purchase items. Mostly jewelry. Connie fingered a few, but she kept touching and retouching a slender silver bracelet with a tiny dangling cross. Just before the clerk rang up his purchases, he pulled one off the display and laid it on the counter. "For my funny, and beautiful, Connie," he said.

"Oh, she must be very special," the clerk responded.

"She is!"

The gray-haired woman smiled warmly looking at Connie. "She is," she said, "and she deserves this." Then she asked, "Engaged?"

Jaeda was flabbergasted. Another E-Ma expression, but in his head. "Uh, not yet," he replied. Connie put a hand to her mouth and turned away. Her face blushing red.

"Sorry," the woman said. "Presumptuous of me. Hope I didn't spoil anything."

~

Jaeda almost felt like going back and kissing the woman. In retrospect, it was an inappropriate question. But somehow it gave him courage. He had expected to be uncomfortable at church, having people look askance at Connie and him because of their different colors. He was stretched out on his bed, Jake prone between his legs, and just thinking. Suddenly, he remembered a phrase Connie and Doreen often used when discussing designs. Color combo! That's what he and Connie were, a color combo. He lifted Jake off to the side and pushed the button on his cell for her.

"We are what?" She sounded confused.

"We are, sweet, funny Connie. That's what we are." He waited, hoping she would get it.

"Uh. I guess."

"I mean us." He hoped his voice was strong and reassuring.

"About designs, fabrics?" She hadn't gotten it yet. So, he prayed.

"Us, Connie, us."

"You mean because I am white and you are black? I don't get it."

Finally he said, "Meet me at Little Corona. I

will explain. Please," he begged.

~

Connie donned her favorite teal sweats. A little heavy, but the beach could get extremely cold in the evening, even the protected one at Little Corona. When she arrived and parked on Poppy Street, she was glad. It was already chilly, and the sea breeze was blowing. She had parked in front of her mother's old friend's quaint beach house. Just three houses away from the path down the steep slope to the small beach. She passed four opulent houses, one blocked by huge trees, all almost touching the path and overlooking the ocean. What would it be like to live in one of these? She had been here many times, but had never seen a human on a porch or even looking out a window. Measuring her steps, she stumbled on a loose stone and almost lost her balance. That's when she felt his arm.

"I am here, Connie. I am here." Hearing him repeat it made her feel safe. But, what was ahead? Why did he want to meet here? Maybe because here is where they had had their first kiss?

Jaeda held her arm firmly, and led her down the steep path. She felt safe. She took off her Converses and wiggled her toes in the sand. She turned to him with questioning eyes.

~

Jaeda looked out at the rolling waves. Seagulls swooped down to grab leftover morsels from the beach. Pelicans sat sentry on floating logs. The sky was bleak, wash water gray. A seal hunkered on a floating jetsam. During the few bay excursions he'd taken with visiting friends, they had seen several seals sunning themselves on discarded floaters and sometimes on floating buoys. He saw this one's mouth open and could almost hear its bark.

Forecasting rain? Maybe he needed to hurry.

Connie was laughing at the gulls and racing toward them to see them skitter and fly away. She was having such a great time he hated to interrupt. He ran to keep up with her and grabbed her hand. She looked at him questioningly, then smiled and squeezed back.

Maybe this was going okay. Maybe he would have the courage. *Please, God, give that to me.* He fingered the tiny box in the pocket of his swimsuit. It was not from the opulent Traditional Jewelers in Fashion Island, but from his dad. It could not be exchanged or even returned. It had been E-Ma's. Dad found it in crumpled tissue when he was going through her things. The worn velvet box had been taped on the bottom to an envelope. The greeting on the address side of the business sized envelope was in his grandmother's ancient scrawl. *To Jaeda for his true love. Wear in love.* Under the flap was a single folded sheet of yellow lined paper. Again in his E-Ma's scribble were these words: *This is for the woman who truly loves you and makes you*

happy and gives me great-grandchildren even if I have to love them from heaven.
E-Ma

PS ~ That is why this is not for Keona.

Oh, boy, E-Ma knew Keona was not the right one for him. But, how? He thought about the times he had brought Keona home to meet his family, especially E-Ma. His then wife was cool and aloof, even dismissed E-Ma like she was a demented old woman, not the matriarch and exceptional lady she was.

He remembered feeling uncomfortable and embarrassed about Keona's behavior, even toward his parents. He chalked it up to nerves. But, he found out later he was wrong. She had tried so hard to make an impression, one that set her above, one that indicated she was more educated, more important than they. He tucked the sour memories back into the pocket of his former life and looked at Funny Connie, the woman who deserved E-Ma's ring.

He loved the cut, the design reminded him of her, pure and simple, no fancy embellishments. He prayed she would love it, too. The stone was the color of Connie's eyes, like the sky on a clear day over the rolling blue waves of the ocean.

She turned to him laughing pointing to the gulls and that silly seal sitting out on the floater. She wrapped her arms around his waist, and he felt her warmth and, hopefully, her love.

Did he have the courage to make his move, to say the words? Maybe if he kissed her like he had that other time on the beach. Maybe.

He tilted her adorable chin and for the first time noticed its dimple. How had he missed that? Probably because he had been concentrating on her beautiful lips. Tracing his finger along the indentation it explored her perfect throat, long and elegant like a snowy egret's. White. Very white. Was that what was holding him back? Her whiteness?

Did God have categories for color? He remembered Connie asking him about Adam and Eve in Genesis. Jaeda closed his eyes and prayed. He pulled the little velvet box out of his trunks and clasped it tightly in his hand. God gave him a nudge. It was now, or maybe never.

CHAPTER TWELVE

*C*onnie thought about doing one of those group phone calls, but she wasn't sure how to do it. Instead, she called Doreen first. She knew Jaeda personally as her co-model and had encouraged Connie to pursue the relationship.

"You're what? You are? How wonderful and exciting." Doreen finished with a "God bless you both."

Next was Noelle and Melanie and good old Natalie who always seemed to be the most available Candy Cane. Cindy and Candy would have to wait since one was in another country and the other on her honeymoon.

She took a picture of her ring and sent it by text

to all. Even to Cindy and Candy. They would get the drift. Then, she decided to be brave and send it to her mom and Sandra. She knew Sandra probably had text, but did her mom?

Tons of questions and requests came back. Send us a photo of him, when is the wedding, tell all. She was overwhelmed, out of her league. Then, she got an idea. She called her friend Peggy, an outstanding photographer who had won awards and taken back cover photos for famous authors. Peggy lived in Corona del Mar. And, she had no problem with mixed color couples. Now, to get Jaeda to agree.

~

Jaeda looked at her request again on email. Why didn't she just call him? So, he called her.
"It will be fun, Jaed. On the beach where we first kissed and where you asked me." He could hear the excitement in her voice. "Bring Jake. He's so cute and really is a part of this."

Jaeda parked his car on Poppy and tucked little Jake under his arm. Was an engagement photo really necessary? Women! Guess he was learning.

He stumbled clumsily down the path to Little Corona Beach expecting to see Connie there. Instead, he was greeted with melodic laughter. "Hi, Jaeda," she said. "I'm Peggy, the photographer." She tossed her gray blonde curls amid more laughter. He had expected to find a silly woman in her twenties, maybe thirties. But, the Peggy woman was maybe old enough to be his mother. After all, she had won many awards. What had he been thinking?

He was cool with that, and with her.

He liked her firm handshake, so she was okay in his book. But, what about all the excited comments and questions? How did he and Connie meet? What was the defining moment in their relationship? Tell her about things they had done together. How did he propose? Where?

He stopped her questions and asked his own whys. She explained knowing more about the couple and their love gave her more insight about how to photograph them. "Make sense?" she asked. She finally asked what he did as a living, as a career. She said she knew all about Connie being a designer, but what about him?

He swallowed hard trying to ignore the basketball sized lump in his throat. Did he have to share about the modeling situation? He decided to tell Peggy about his real career as a manager at a bank. She picked up on that. So, he guessed it all okay. Was it?

Jake barked an announcement. Jaeda tried to reassure him, but the little dog stumbled up the pathway kicking pebbles and stones behind him. Peggy laughed and said, "So cute. He must love her, too."

Connie raised her arms up and giggled. She was attired in the wispy skirt she had worn the night they danced at the Pavilion. She teetered at the top of the pebbly path and reached down to pet the little dog behind his ears. She looked adorable, and Jaeda almost lost it. She was carrying her fancy silver shoes dangling from a hand. He raced up to meet her to guide her down. Instead, he scooped her up and carried her. Jake nipped at his heels as the sentry. Jaeda hadn't realized the dog cared so much for Connie. Was he hoping she would be his new mother?

Peggy laughed loudly, even clapped her hands and hooted, then brought her camera up to her face and started clicking. When he gently placed Connie down on the sand, he noticed Peggy's eyes were misty. That, and her warm embrace of Connie, sealed the deal for him. He might even share about the modeling part.

~

Connie collapsed on her bed. The photo occasion was even more draining than the actual proposal. Well, maybe not, but it was challenging. Maybe it was all the questions Peggy had asked. She was an outstanding photographer and wanted to understand her subjects. But, Connie had been reluctant to share about Jaeda's modeling. He had, too.

Still, Peggy somehow sensed the omission.

Finally, Connie whispered in her ear and explained. Peggy nodded, said "I understand. Trust, girl." Peggy would write the engagement notice to be put in the local papers, but she would send it to Connie first for editing and affirmation.

So, what was troubling her? Was she still hung up on the color of skin thing? Was Jaeda? She hadn't heard back from Sandra. That worried her. Sisters were supposed to support each other, weren't they?

~

Jaeda called his mom. Emailing or texting wasn't her thing at her age. Not that she was that old, but she was from a different era. He had tried before and had gotten no response. Sissy told him to forget it, just call. He held his breath waiting for Mom to pick up the phone. Instead, he got Dad.

"Hey, Son! What's up? Tell all." Dad was so upfront, really did want Jaeda to tell all. So, grabbing the proverbial bull by the long horns, he did.

"You are? You really are?" Dad sounded excited. "'bout time, boy. We want more grandchildren." His laughter was warm, so Jaeda jumped in.

"You remember Connie the girl I brought to New York for E-Ma's funeral?"

"Sure do. Stunner. Pretty girl, very gracious." Dad paused and cleared his throat. "She the one?"

"Yes." That was the simple direct answer. Then, "You okay with that?"

"Why? 'Cause she's white?" Dad was always direct. Jaeda liked that.

"Son, I don't care if she's purple as long as you love her, and she loves you."

Jaeda almost dropped the phone he was so relieved. "But, Dad, what about the others? What about Mom?" He had to ask, he had to know.

"Sniff and boodle. Who cares as long as you both love each other." Dad's funny ancient expression caught Jaeda in a laughing fit, almost. He swallowed his mirth and loved his dad more for it.

"Dad," he was reluctant to ask, but had to know. "Have there been any mixed marriages before, in our family?" He rubbed his nose and waited for the reply.

"Mmm. Seems to me a few. Long ago. Oh, maybe Aunt Sophie? Gotta ask your mother."

Jaeda waited. Dad had put the phone down. Now, he would be interrogated by Mom. Could he handle that? He prayed.

CHAPTER THIRTEEN

"She said what?" Connie held the phone closer to her ear even though it was on speaker. She wanted to hear his words loud.

"She sends her blessing. Dad does, too. In spades." Oops, maybe an inappropriate analogy. He grinned to himself and took a deep cleansing breath. "They love you. You made a great impression at E-Ma's funeral. They don't care if you are purple or white."

"Oh, Jaeda, I am so happy. For us." She shifted position on the bed, crossed her ankles and wiggled her toes. Time for a pedi. The sparkling stuff was wearing off, and she was tired of blue. She would call Tammy tomorrow.

"Jae?" She had started calling him by that nickname, and he didn't seem to object.

"Mmm?" They were on Facetime on their phones, and she saw him pinch the bridge of his nose. Cute gesture. "What, my funny Connie?"

"Peggy called. She is sending me several, actually about twenty, photos in my email for us to choose from. I want you to help decide."

"Okay. Is the Jakester in them?"

She laughed. "Of course. And he will probably steal the show."

~

They decided to meet for lunch. They had never done that before. Connie wondered why. It had always been coffee at Starbucks. Since they both loved sushi, they met at Kitayama not too far from Fashion Island where the bank was. Connie loved to sit at the sushi bar, because she loved watching the sushi chefs prepare the delicacies, but Jaeda asked for one of the small, intimate tables tucked in the back. Better, she agreed, to hold hands and snuggle. They placed their order for sashimi, and while waiting for their soup, Connie brought up her email with all the engagement photos. Just as she thought, Jaeda picked the one where Jake looked the cutest. "But, I look so windblown!"

"You look adorable. As usual," he grinned.

"But, my hair!"

"I love it that way. So free and natural. Keona

always had those kinky, tight curls." He pinched his nose.

Awe. Oh. She was being compared to his ex, his black ex, yet. She twisted in her seat and tried to look him formidably in his dark brown eyes, but his lids were lowered, and there was a faint blush on his cheeks above the recent Hawaii Five-O stubble that she decided she loved.

"Sorry. Bad comment." Jaeda slid out of the booth, grabbed her hand and pulled her toward him. "Let's get out of here," he said firmly. He left the rest of his salmon sashimi sitting lonely on his plate.

~

Little Corona Beach looked the same, abandoned. No surfers because it was not a surfing beach. She guessed the waves weren't high enough, or something about the tide she didn't understand. Beautiful shells still littered the sand begging to be picked up and saved. But, she couldn't since the beach was a protected environment. A lone seal sat out on a piece of jetsam an howled. Should she feel sorry for him or happy he had found some private time? Not many gulls dove on the beach tonight. Since so few families picnicked in this area, there were seldom leftovers. Big Corona Beach had the most trash from all the parties and cookouts and kids' sports teams' getogethers. But, Little Corona was almost private, secluded. Just for her and Jaeda.

They had parked his car up on Poppy Street and

scrambled their way down the path past the four huge houses, the ones no one ever seemed to live in or stand out on a balcony to watch the beauty of the waves and the sunset. He held her silver sandals dangling from his hand.

This time it was just the two of them. No photographer, no cute little dog. Just them. Jaeda drew her into his arms, and she snuggled resting her chin on his heartbeat. She lifted her face to question him.

"It is right, Funny Connie, it is right," he said. He tilted her chin to kiss it delicately, then without warning, he placed his full lips on hers and gave her the kiss of a lifetime.

~

Connie would never forget that kiss. Her knees still felt wobbly, even though she was lying sprawled on her bed. She had never been kissed so passionately before, especially by a male model. She giggled at that thought, then got so hysterical with laughter she had to hold her tummy. She mustn't tell Jaeda that she had categorized him as male model, not banker. But, that is actually how their relationship that developed into romance began. She had memory flashes of him standing on the pedestal draped in plaid with Jake under his arm. He had looked pretty silly. Even Doreen was holding her laughter at bay; she could tell by the smirk on her face and her quivering lips.

Jaeda had been a good sport, mostly because he was trying to make up for the financial mistake when he had helped her with her budget from the Memory Men windfall. He stood for numerous fittings, even being poked with pins by Alice, and all for free. As a result, Connie was able to tell Doug, her then boss, she would not need, nor accept, the latest male model he had reserved for her. Jaeda was volunteering she told him.

Doug had asked some inappropriate questions. "He gay? What's his deal? Wants free publicity? Sex?"

She was tempted to slap him, then decided he wasn't worth the effort to raise her hand. She had handed him her resignation from Nature's Bounty, turned on her silver heels and walked out. Fortunately, her contract stated she could use the same room for fittings for another six months. Perfect. By then she will have moved into her new studio.

~

Jaeda smacked himself hard. His face stung, but he didn't care. He looked in the mirror. Yep, a big handprint on his brown skin. Would he ever learn? Why had he even mentioned Keona's name? She was so in the past, but she was, unfortunately, part of it. For six years.

He was stewing, pacing from one end of his living room to the other. Then to the kitchen and opening the fridge to find it empty. At least of anything edible. He was about to call Connie to go even to McDonald's for a burger when his cell chimed. Gotta get rid of the drum beats. He didn't pay attention to the caller ID and picked it up with "Hi, Con."

"Who is Con?" the belligerent voice on the other end asked.

"Oh, Keona."

"That's me."

"What do you want?" He was tempted to hang up, but she hadn't called in five months. Maybe there was something wrong with one of her parents, both of whom he really liked.

"Changed my mind. I want to get back together." Her voice was raspy, but she sounded resolute and a little tipsy. "Just get rid of the stupid dog."

"Who left the light one?" He almost spit it out. It was an old saying they'd had to bring arguments or difficult situations to the forefront, out in the open. She was asking for permission to bring up old wounds. He would not give it.

"Goodbye, Keona! It is over. Forever."

"Not so fast, Sexy Jae-Jae. I am outside and will not leave."

He was pretty sure he had never gotten the key back from her, and he had foolishly never changed the locks. He slapped himself again, this time on his head.

"Do not come into this house. I mean it."

"Already here, darlin', already here."

He spun from the kitchen. She was leaning provocatively on the sideboard, like a hussy, or a call girl. Like a woman trying to entice him with sex.

"Wow," she said. "You still got it Mr. Sexy Man." She wiggled her body and taking short, deliberate steps in her platform high heels, she crept toward him. "You know you can't resist me," she said. "And what we had. Fantastic!" She drew the word out seductively – watching his face the whole time.

Jaeda needed strength. He prayed for it, then called Connie. "Please come right over, please," he pleaded.

~

Connie threw her phone down in haste, then thinking more clearly stuffed it into her purse. Jaeda's voice echoed in her ears as she raced to her little car and gunned the engine. He sounded desperate, yet she didn't know why. She knew if he had been confronted by a robber he would never call her and ask her to come. He would never put her in danger. But, why had he called and practically shouted, pleading in desperation?

She zoomed up into his driveway, jerked her car into park and jumped out grapping her bag.

That's when she noticed the Jag next to hers in the double driveway. It was silver, sleek and still purring from the intense summer heat. Her mind did tailspins until she remembered the one conversation they'd had about his ex. "Very controlling. Doesn't give up, not easily." She also remembered Keona had a luxury sport car.

Connie made a decision, one that would change everything, she hoped, then she prayed. She almost kicked in the front door, then realized it was half open. She was on a roll to save her man.

She entered shouting, "I have a gun, and I am not afraid to use it."

Jaeda looked at her, confusion on his face, then he broke into a wide smile. "Connie," he said calmly, "meet Keona."

The other woman sidled up to him and threw her arms around him in a demonstration of possession. How could he be so calm? Or, was this other woman in a control mode that she had learned in six years? Had she literally mesmerized him? Was she evil?

Connie patted her purse. "Gun." Jaeda looked cockeyed at her. Then she saw the wicked sparks in Keona's eyes. She pulled out her pistol and aimed it.

~

Little Jake was anchored at Jaeda's feet, his tiny canine body wiggling, but not with pleasure.

His sharp, staccato barks made Connie realize he was in defensive mode. Jaeda tried to bend down to pick up the little dog, but the woman clinging to his arm stopped him.

"Leave the stupid mutt alone," she said, her voice laced with nasty. Her face screwed up. Her eyes were bare slits and her mouth contorted. Without warning she kicked hard at the little dog sending him across the room. He lay on his side whimpering, his almond eyes pleading to Jaeda.

That did it for Connie. She loved Jake, knew how much Jaeda loved him, and she couldn't stand cruelty. She clicked the trigger on her gun and fired.

The sultry woman's eyes got huge. Connie hoped she was frightened. No, scared to death. Because that's what Connie wanted for her. Death.

CHAPTER FOURTEEN

*J*aeda laid a cool cloth on her forehead. She reached for it and flung it off. Why had she fainted? She remembered pulling the trigger and the little gun with the pink handle vibrating in her hand. Then, all was lost.

"What happened? Did I kill her?"

Jaeda laughed. "No. But you scared the poop out of her. Literally."

Lying on his sofa, she turned her head and noticed him wiping up a dark spot on his carpet. How could that be? His carpet was brown, yet a yukky spot was there. She felt terrible, but at the same time gleeful. "Really? She really had an accident? Because of me?"

This time he laughed so loud she almost had to hold her ears. "Keona," he said, rather matter of factly, "always had some incontinence problems. I had to clean up a few times. Actually, many." He grinned at Connie and placed the cool cloth on her forehead again.

~

"I can't believe I did that, actually fired my gun." She grinned at Jaeda. "Did I?"

He nodded. "Yes, you fired. Bad aim, though. Fortunately."

"Where, what did I hit? Or, did I hit?"

He sighed and took her hand. "You hit my fifty-four inch TV. Smashed it to oblivion."

"Oh. Bad move. So sorry. I will replace." That was all she could say when her voice and energy gave out. Then, she fell into a deep sleep dreaming about holding the little pink-handled revolver and pressing the trigger and smacking that horrible woman in the face.

"You are a slut," a voice said. "No, you are the slut," another other voice said. "He's mine, always will be," the first voice shouted. "No, he's mine now," the other voice responded.

Connie rubbed her eyes with a damp hand and moved her head back and forth on the sofa pillow. What had happened here in Jaeda's living room? She tried to remember, but it was fuzzy.

Jaeda was holding her hand. He was crouched

on the carpet next to the sofa. His eyes held, what? Concern?

Her first waking thought was for the dog. "Jake?"

"He is fine," Jaeda said as he lifted the little dog up to her. Jake wiggled and leaned toward her whining and sticking out his tiny tongue licking. He wanted to kiss her!

"But, she was so mean to him," she said. "Kicking him viciously. I can't even imagine doing that. I couldn't, ever.

"Is he hurt?" Connie worried about Jake being kicked hard, so hard he ended up across the room. After all, he was a little dog, not bigger than her purse. She reached for the dog and cuddled him close to her chest where he snuggled. "You all right, Jakester?" she asked as the tiny tongue explored her chin. She laughed at the tickling sensation and snuggled him closer. She had found a new friend, hopefully for life.

"So," she was reluctant to ask, but had to know. "What exactly happened? Like, where is she now? Where did she go?" Connie struggled with the questions, but she had to know, and felt like she deserved the answers. Apparently, Jaeda agreed.

"After her 'accident', you get my drift I'm sure, she swore at both of us and high-tailed it out of here. Last I heard was the loud sound of her car engine." He turned to Connie and grinned.

But, she wasn't convinced. Women like Keona didn't just disappear into the fog. They filtered through it and wispy-like found their way back again and again. They were enigmas who didn't take no for answers, who never left their prey alone. Ever.

~

Connie needed her sisters, her Candy Cane sisters. She figured out a way to make a group call, at least to those in the states. Maybe with Cindy's new phone that had a California prefix, she could be included. She dialed.

Hearing several voices at once was confusing. Finally getting it straight, and shouting instructions, they understood. It was as if they were sitting down together to share and pray.

Connie took charge since she was the initiator of the call. She explained what had taken place at Jaeda's and their relationship. She heard lots of "Oos and Awes."

Finally, Cindy, the strong one, said, "Let us pray."

"Dear Heavenly Father," she said. "Thank You for your strength and love, and thank You for not having any discernment about color or ethnicity or any physical differences between us. Thank you for giving us Adam and Eve. We have no idea what color they were because you never shared that with us. So, Father, please bless Connie and Jaeda, keep them safe from all harm, and bring them complete happiness. In Your Holy Name. Amen."

Connie was blown away. Cindy was so such a minister, and her prayers were so powerful. She would plant that church in Costa Rica. Connie was sure. She put her phone down, pulled up the covers and surrendered to a restful sleep.

CHAPTER FIFTEEN

*C*onnie directed the 2 Guys Movers as they hoisted her old sofa up the stairs. She had given serious thought to replacing the furniture from her little house in Costa Mesa for new, fun stuff for the loft in Corona del Mar. But, she was on a frugal streak. Even with Jaeda's donation of time modeling, and a few extra bucks in the coffers from her Memory Men windfall, she was trying to be prudent and wanted to feel secure for whatever the future might bring for her business, and for her and Jaeda.

Them.

She brushed her bangs aside in the heat and dreamed. Her gown was already designed, the engraved invitations mailed, the Balboa Pavilion reserved and as were the reservations at the Westin Kierland in Scottsdale for their honeymoon. Jaeda was so excited to introduce her to his new city. He had been there for over a month in his new position as bank manager for the bank's biggest branch. He rode his cycle back every other weekend to help with the wedding planning, had rented a townhome in Scottsdale Ranch in an exclusive little community, only 145 homes, with a real human being at a real guard gate house. They would even pick up their mail there.

Jaeda said Jake loves it, too. It was a real dog-loving community. Their little home was on a cul-de-sac with only fifteen others, and at least eight had dogs. Jake had already been introduced to Prince the poodle next door and Zoe the Miniature Schnauzer on the other side. He had ridden the almost four hundred miles from California to Arizona and back in the sidecar of the cycle twice and loved the wind blowing in his tiny face. He was a good traveler. It was settled.

Was it?

Connie wasn't used to giving up control. She had spent so many years struggling to establish her design business, making her mark in the tenuous fashion world. She was grateful for Doug the Dog's support and his belief in her, and he had finally smiled and bitten his bottom lip almost raw agreeing to let her off the hook. He even mumbled something about her creativity and wished her success. Alice would stay with her to keep doing her pinning and sizing and cutting, and grinning up at tall Jaeda with a gleam in her eye. Doreen vowed her allegiance, so she would continue to model for the disability line. All was good. Maybe.

~

Jaeda adjusted his helmet and settled Jake in the blanket in the sidecar. Both of them loved the freedom of riding and the wind in their hair. Well, the wind on Jaeda's scalp since his head was shaved. He chuckled at the vision of no hair, and under his helmet. Then he thought about the few times Connie had sat behind him with her hair escaping and blowing in billows from underneath the confines of her helmet. Once in a while, he could glance back at her and see brown wisp's flying. But, because of the visor on the helmet, he could never see her eyes. Only feel her hands and arms gripping his body.

"Off to Newport, little guy!" He patted Jake on the head and gunned it.

~

Connie sighed a lot these days. Why was she worried? This should be the happiest time in her life. She loved weddings, had been in many, especially Candy Cane ones. Had even designed the gowns for each of the brides. This time it was her turn.

Melanie and Natalie met her at the Pavilion to discuss details with the venue's event coordinator. She shook the woman's hand and turned to her Candy Cane sisters. "I need Jill."

Natalie's eyebrows rose into peaks. "You mean Jill who went with us to Costa Rica for Cindy's wedding?"

"Yes. She also helped with Noelle's, even Candy's. I need her calm expertise, her input and advice."

"Then," Melanie said, "let's get out of here and call her."

~

Jill was flabbergasted. Another Candy Cane wedding? Unfortunately, she had a commitment for a wedding at a huge hotel in Dana Point. What could she do? She loved all the Candy Cane girls, but she had signed a contract with the other couple and the woman's mother who was paying. She was a professional and couldn't break a contract. The only one she had ever agreed to extend was Noelle Day's.

Hers was a special case, and Jill couldn't tolerate abuse. So, she had agreed to keep the deposit and hold it until a time when Noelle found the real Mr. Right who treated her right. When it finally happened with Braydon Lovejoy, Jill was thrilled. Plus, she had never coordinated a wedding in The Sherman Foundation Gardens. It was a first for her, and turned out to be a fun challenge.

Jill looked over the current contract again. No glitches, no opt outs. She repeated her grandmother's phrases out loud to herself. "What will be, will be." And one of her favorites, "Things will all work out, dear." She hoped so and went to bed.

~

Connie grabbed the offending phone and almost threw it. She blinked her eyes and looked at the ergonomic clock displaying five-thirty. In the morning? Who at this absurd time? She never looked at the caller I.D. hoping it was Jaeda. Or, worried it might be that nasty, angry Keona.

The voice on the other end was excited. She finally identified it. Jill?

"I can hardly believe it. The mother of the bride called me to cancel."

What? Who? Connie didn't understand. But, Jill explained.

"It's a family thing, an ethnicity thing. The groom's parents aren't happy with his choice of a bride. So," she went on, "their wedding is cancelled." There was a dramatic pause, and Connie could hear Jill's rapid breathing. "You still want me?"

Connie sat up straight in bed and shook her head to rid it of the fog in her brain. Of course she wanted Jill; didn't know why she hadn't asked her before. Why had she been such a control freak to think she could do the whole wedding herself?

"Oh, yes, yes! Please. When can you start to help me?"

"How about today? Can we meet for coffee and you bring all the details and vendors you have contracted with for flowers and food and anything else you can think of?"

~

Connie placed a file folder in front of Jill on her usual Starbucks table. She felt as if she should pay rent on it.

Jill flipped through the folder and said, "Really?" She rolled her eyes and sighed. "Obviously you will get your flowers from Love In Joy, the Lovejoy's floral shop. That is perfect. But, what about the caterer? You really serious about this one? Have you put down a deposit?" She scanned the printed pages and groaned. "Not them, surely? Can you get the deposit back?

"Who's doing the cake? Did you find one you like on a wedding site and give them a photo?"

Connie felt so inadequate listening to Jill's questions. She knew she had raced through decisions and hadn't read all the contracts thoroughly. Since the wedding was still three weeks away, maybe something could be done to correct her hasty errors.

~

What had she done? Or, more specifically, not done? Connie collapsed on her red sofa and called Jaeda. He sounded excited to hear from her, but she was weepy. She felt like such a failure. Here she was a now almost noted fashion designer, but she couldn't plan her own wedding without glitches. What, she wondered, happened to the days when brides' mothers helped, even made decisions? Well, that wouldn't happen with her mom who would only criticize and have a handy Bible verse to support her disapproval and her pre-formed opinions.

What, too, about her parents' and her mom's attitude about Connie marrying out of her color? Sandra had been supportive, but neither of them had approached Mom about the fact that Jaeda's skin was dark, a lot darker than Connie's. Her parents would be coming to the wedding with expectations very different from what they would see. Dad was excited to guide her down the aisle. Yet, he had never met Jaeda. She had sent photos, but did they look at them carefully? Maybe it was time for a family visit.

CHAPTER SIXTEEN

"*J*ae, take off that ridiculous tie. You don't have to be formal in front of my parents."

He scowled at her, removed the tie and folded it carefully to tuck in his jacket pocket. "Okay now?"

"Yes, thank you. And try to remember how scared I was meeting your parents a few months ago. It wasn't easy for me."

Sandra met them at the airport in the luggage retrieval area. She bounced up and down like a kid winning a soccer match. Connie and she threw their arms around each other squeezing hard. They both needed that.

After kissing and hugging, Sandra looked

beyond Connie. Was she surprised? Surely, she knew about Jaeda being African-American. But her face tilted up high to the tall black man. Then she hugged him, reaching only to his shoulders, and Connie felt okay. It was all going to be okay. Or, was it?

~

"Oh," Mom said as she grasped his hand. "You are taller than I expected." Still, she smiled and held his hand tightly. That was a start.

Dad gave him the guy hug and the pounding on the back thing. Never said a word about Jaeda's skin color. But, Jeff, her brother-in-law, Sandra's husband, did.

"I don't know how to, but I apologize for Jeff. He was so out of line." She looked at Jaeda's face. He seemed fine.

"He was honest, has his diversity problems. Can't fault him for that. It happens."

How she loved this man for being so accepting and understanding. She chalked Jeff's comments to human frailty.

They were eating dessert after her mother's yummy enchiladas. Jaeda had taken a second helping and loaded his up with sour cream and Mom's homemade guacamole. My, that man could eat! And she couldn't cook, but barely. The dessert was Mom's special Bundt cake soaked in orange juice. They all groaned but ate every bite on their plates. Even Jeff sucked it up while claiming he couldn't eat another bite of anything.

They had moved into the living room, mugs of coffee in hands. Mom finally had the courage to bring up 'the subject.' Dad just nodded and smiled; so did Sandra and, thankfully, Jeff. Maybe he had gotten the 'talking' from Sandra.

"So," she hesitated taking a breath. "How exactly did you two meet?"

Connie said a silent prayer of thanks for Mom's courage.

Then, Jaeda took the legendary bull by the horns. He was her Jacob! Although he hadn't waited for fourteen years to win Connie, he had waited almost fourteen months. He explained, nodding to Connie for affirmation, about the Memory Men and how they had gifted Connie's entrepreneurial efforts. He even shared a sketchy and rather dramatic, Connie thought, account of their first date at the Balboa Pavilion, and the others on Little Corona Beach. Apparently, he wanted to confirm how special their relationship was, how special he felt about Connie. She nodded and blushed, noticed he did, too. It did show through his skin color.

After a losing game of chess with her dad, Jaeda went back to the hotel. Connie slept in her old room, sans Sandra. So many memories; teen posters and wall colors she would never have chosen now at twenty-eight. She found her old diary in a drawer. It looked as if no one had opened it for ten years. Had Mom been that honoring of her secrets? Flipping through it, she found a tattered post-it. "Bless you, daughter," it said simply. Mom had found it, but did honor at least a part of her scribblings. It was dated almost ten years ago.

~

Jaeda and Connie stood in the long security line at the airport. Denver didn't seem quite as frustrating as Phoenix, but close. She was ahead of Jaeda, but turned when she heard the TSA woman questioning him. "You the one in the U Tube adds? In the plaid?" She asked him another question, very brief since it was a long security line. "She the designer?" She gestured to Connie.

Jaeda grinned and nodded.

CHAPTER SEVENTEEN

*J*ill set things in motion, and Connie got her security deposits back. The wedding was only two weeks away, so both Jill and Connie had to hustle. "How can we salvage these horrible and hasty mistakes I made?"

"I know you, Connie. You want everything perfect," Jill quipped. Connie nodded with misty eyes.

"I got ahead of myself and blew it." She grasped Jill's hand across the now almost rented Starbucks table. "My biggest concern, other than the obvious gown, cake, food, music and ceremony," she said laughing, "is his family. I want it to be special for them, too. But, I don't want them

133

to think of me, or see me, as a bossy, bitchy, controlling white girl. I am me, and I want them to see me that way. Just me."

"I understand," Jill said as she nodded. "I agree. But, I do have one suggestion that might help your design business. Wanna hear it?"

~

Jill found a super cute young guy who did a U Tube video. It featured Connie's wedding gown designs and the attire of the attendants. The venue and other parts of the wedding-to-be were not included. But, the gown designs got so many responses it put Winning Designs on the map. No other advertising was necessary. Best part, it paid for the expensive wedding.

~

Jaeda called. "Two of my coworkers saw a U Tube video that promoted our wedding. What was that about?"

"Not our wedding, Silly. Just a promotion about my wedding designs. You will not see my gown until I walk down the aisle."

CHAPTER EIGHTEEN

Sandra called Connie. She was either beside herself with glee, or she was having some kind of fit. Connie opted for the former. She tried to remain calm.

"Con! This is fantastic! You have hit the big time. You are a star." Sandra went on, bubbling, babbling and confusing her words, but it made Connie feel warm and mushy inside. She was a good sister. Connie needed to feel that. Sandra, the daughter who had fulfilled Mom's dreams to be a stay at home mom and provide their parents with grandchildren.

"Con," she said after a pause, "have you thought about, considered, a maternity line?"

"You are expecting again?" Connie asked, hopeful.

"Yeh, in five more months." She paused to catch a breath. "Can you? Could you? I have so many women in my Bible study, all pg. They would lap up your designs."

This was overwhelming, over the top. She was planning a wedding, hers. Still, the opportunity to expand, as it had done with Doreen's disability, energized her. Could she do it?

~

Jaeda jumped on his cycle, adjusted his helmet and revved it up. The sound of the motor soothed him, helped him think. So many questions. What kind of wedding was Connie planning? He had left most of the details up to her. Wasn't it the bride who cared about color and timing and food? Even seating arrangements?

He had finally met with Jill the wedding coordinator last weekend when he was in Newport. She emphasized seating at the reception, the timing of the dances and speeches and the cake cutting. Thank goodness the wind was blowing against the visor of his helmet to distract him. He had really liked Jill a lot. After all, she had helped Noelle and Cindy and Candy with their wedding preparations, even flown to Costa Rica for Cindy's.

But, she scared him when she ticked off a list of what his expectations were. The worst of which was dancing with Connie's mom. Even though they'd had a good visit in Denver, he felt she wasn't really comfortable with him for a son-in-law. He feared the woman despised him because of his color. But, her sister Sandra said Mabel Winfield had come around. According to Sandra, Mrs. Winfield was more interested in grandchildren than what color they were.

~

Connie tried to reassure him. They were seated at what she now definitely called her rented table at Starbucks. He looked confused, and weary from his five plus hour ride from Arizona to Newport even on his super speedy cycle. She gave a delicate touch to his hand. Would her love for him come through her fingertips?

He grinned and rubbed the new stubble on his face. She said she wasn't so sure about it, the Hawaii Five-O look, but it did exude sexiness. And, in her book, he was sexy.

"Mom's not so bad," she said. "She is traditional. Maybe, in some ways, your mom is, too?"

The comment and question hung in the air between a latte and a Frappuccino.

~

Jaeda thought about Connie's comment about his mom and nodded. "You met her. What did you think?" he said throwing the gauntlet back to her.

"I think, mmm," she locked her eyes to his, "she is adorable. I would love to have her as a mother-in-law and a friend. Actually," she continued staring at him, "I think if they got to know each other, our mothers could be great friends."

"You do?"

"Yes. They are both strong Christians; both attend Bible study and both love their children. And," she chuckled, "both want more grandchildren." She noticed his eyes twinkled. "That good enough for you?"

"Well, it's good enough for me," Jill said as she slipped into the chair next to Connie. "Sorry if I was eavesdropping a bit, but I couldn't resist as I approached you two lovebirds." She slapped a file folder on the table. "Now, to business, or even busyness. Lots to do in a short time."

Each had an assignment. Jaeda blanched a bit when he heard his part. He still hadn't asked any of his friends or co-workers to be attendants. The wedding was only weeks away. Who would he ask? Who would agree and be happy for him and willing to fork out the money for a tux? Tomorrow he would find out.

~

Jill left them with lists, a venti Frappuccino in her hand and a check from Connie for the caterers. Connie would pay Love In Joy directly for the flowers since they had agreed on a price, and it was owned by Rob's and Braydon's mom. She had some reservations about the caterers. Jill recommended them highly, and she trusted Jill's judgement. After all, she had been a wedding coordinator for over twenty years. Surely, she would know.

When she got home she called Jill with her concerns. "Can they do traditional Southern dishes? Sort of in honor to E-Ma?"

"This is your opportunity," Jill said, "to connect with his mom. Ask her for advice and suggestions.

"But," Jill concluded, "remember E-Ma is dead, and this is Jaeda's and your wedding, not hers." Connie heard the phone click. Guess Jill was over her peevishness tonight. One thing she didn't want to be was a Bridezilla.

~

The somewhat halted conversation with Jaeda's mom turned out okay. Connie had been such a wreck when she called, but his mom was sweet and gracious and very excited. She also said how grateful she was that Connie was asking advice.

When Connie hung up she realized she still didn't know the woman's first name. Nor, his dad's. Surely, when they had been introduced in New York she had heard both. Maybe her brain was fried from stewing over wedding decisions. No, fried would be sizzled. She called Doreen. She needed centering help.

CHAPTER NINETEEN

*I*t was two-fifteen. She didn't want to talk with anyone, even Jaeda, at the ungodly hour. She hit the cellphone on the little nightstand next to her bed so many times she hoped she had killed it. No way.

Rubbing her eyes until they hurt, she finally picked it up after probably the third call from whomever. When she heard the news she coughed into a tissue uncontrollably. Sitting up straight and gathering her senses, she said, "So sorry. What?"

"Connie, that you? It's Rob. We had our baby!"

"What? Really?" She wasn't making sense, then she understood. Cindy's baby, Rob's. When it actually computed all she could think about was the fact she was an aunt again. Another Candy Cane had been blessed.

~

The next morning the phone lines between seven women buzzed. Connie was grateful she had figured out how to make group phone calls. Everyone chattered at once. Even Noelle took a leave from her class and had passed it on to a sub teacher. So had Melanie from her preschool students.

Nat almost closed the gym, then decided to leave it in the capable hands of Bryce her personal trainer at the gym. She went home to sprawl on her sofa and soak up all the latest news. Candy and Devin were in the airport waiting for their flight home from their honeymoon. Doreen, like Connie, woke up from a deep sleep, but was ready and raring to go to learn all about the first Candy Cane baby.

Rob was so excited he almost burst through the phone lines. In minutes, his mom and dad entered the wild conversation, as well as Cindy's dad. Connie wondered how she had done that, but, no matter, it was wonderful and special. Then, they heard a baby's cry. Had everyone burst into tears as she had?

"That," Rob said, "was little Robbie. He has a big voice."

Robinson Logan Lovejoy was eight pounds, seven ounces; healthy and with all fingers and toes, even a grin. Life felt complete for all the Candy Cane sisters, except for Connie who still needed to plan a wedding.

CHAPTER TWENTY

$\mathcal{N}$ine women gathered and giggled in Connie's new studio. All except the bride were attired in gauzy sea green dresses, some to their ankles, a few only to their knees. The gowns were all identical except for the lengths. Doreen's was long with a split skirt on the side opposite her shorter leg so the longer side would camouflage her lift shoe. Connie was glad she had purchased a special pair of shoes for Doreen in silver to match all the other girls and hers. All their fingertips, toes too, were adorned with silver glitter, a Kay specialty from Pauline's Nails.

Connie had decided silver was her signature color after she had worn her silver sandals to dance in the night when she and Jaeda went to the Balboa Pavilion. She was sure that was the night she almost fell in love with him.

She would never presume to insist her mother and Jaeda's mom all wear silver, but she suggested ideas for silver adornments. Both chose soft, floating dresses with either silver adorned necklines or silver jewelry, and both had found silver pumps and tiny silver clutch bags. Braydon Lovejoy had once again outdone the flowers. The two mothers wore white rose corsages dusted in glittering silver with a pearl in the center of each of the three roses; the Candy Canes and the other attendants carried bouquets of 50 Shades of Early Grey roses. Connie got a kick out of the name, a relatively new addition to the rose family. The outer petals of the delicate blooms were the faintest blush green complimenting the bridesmaids' aquamarine gowns.

Connie's bridal bouquet was magnificent. She had always dreamed of a cascading bouquet, but when Braydon presented her with a round one that looked like a huge pouf of white roses she gasped. "There are three dozen," he said, "and each rose has a pearl in the middle, and those sprigs of tiny silver balls tucked in between the roses are berries I sprayed. The stems form a handle wrapped in six silver ribbons tied in French knots with a pearl on each knot." He grinned. "You do have six attendants, right?"

She fingered the creamy pearls at her neck, the ones Jaeda's mother had given her. "Yes," she nodded and dabbed a tissue to the corners of her eyes. "How perfect, Braydon, how perfect."

She didn't have the heart to remind him Sandra her sister and Jaeda's sister Valerie were also attendants. Then she realized the six other Candy Canes were super special, always would be. The silver ribbons symbolized them.

EPILOGUE

$\mathcal{T}$hree white limousines pulled up to the Harborside Grand Ballroom at the Balboa Pavilion. A tourist stood on the sidewalk and rubbed his eyes. He started counting. Eight beautiful women in sea-colored gowns and a woman in sparkling white. Must be a bride? Then two older women who clasped hands. Onc was dark brown, the other white. But, they smiled at each other and hugged. The younger women, how many again?, all carried beautiful bouquets. Must be a wedding. He pulled up the camera on his cell phone, had to share this with his wife and daughter in Omaha. The woman next to him said, "Ain't this special? We are witnessing a weddin'." He nodded and clicked.

Connie shifted her feet in her silver sandals. She probably should have worn pumps, but the sandals were the same ones she wore with Jaeda at the beach so many times. Especially during their first dance, first kiss and their engagement. She adjusted the elegant comb in her hair, E-Ma's special comb. She thought E-Ma had been buried with it. But, when Jaeda's mom sent it to her UPS, she was thrilled with the special gift.

The pre-wedding music started with Blue Moon. She would no longer be standing alone, now she had a dream in her heart. Connie clutched her father's bent arm. He patted her hand and whispered in her ear. "I am so proud of you, and so thrilled you found the man of your dreams. He is a good man." George Winfield stopped just as his eyes clouded with tears. He almost started down the aisle with her until she reminded him the attendants went first. He laughed silently and patted her hand again.

Noelle, Melanie, Natalie, Cindy, Candy and Valerie drifted like clouds down the white runner. Cindy had made a special trip back to California. Rob's mother, Lydia, held baby Robby in her arms. Rob was standing close to Jaeda as an attendant.

Doreen practically floated in her special gown. No one who didn't know would suspect her disability. Finally came Sandra, her precious sister and now her best friend again. Sandra was a bit pudgy from having all those babies and expecting again, but she looked glowing. Connie hoped she would someday glow like that, too, for the same reason. Then came Missy, Jaeda's sister with a huge smile on her face. All looked so radiant, almost ethereal in the gowns Connie had designed.

All during the bridesmaids' entrances Connie's eyes were glued to her groom who seemed a million miles away in front of the improvised alter. Jaeda was standing stock still except for fiddling with his cuff links. What? She knew he favored the outdated jewelry, but really? In a modern tux? He had hinted at a surprise for her, but she hadn't seen one yet. Surely, not him wearing cuff links.

Now the music switched from Blue Moon to the traditional wedding march. It was Dad's and her turn, and her normally firm legs started to wobble. "You okay, baby girl?" Dad asked. Worry wrinkled his brow.

"Yes, Daddy. Okay. Just filled with joy." He squeezed her hand clutched in the bend of his arm, kissed her on her nose like he had done when she was a child, and led her forward.

Pastor Tom conducted the ceremony. He had been her first choice, the one she had counseled with when she was uncertain about her relationship with Jaeda. He seemed to have a glean in his eye when it came to the exchange of the rings. Sandra had her ring for Jaeda nestled in her bouquet, and she expected Jaeda's brother-in-law Sean to have hers in his pocket. They had decided on no ring bearers because the only ones at the right age were Sandra's children, and it was too expensive to fly them to California.

When Pastor Tom asked for the ring for Connie from Jaeda, he hesitated and put his fingers to his lips. A shrill whistle startled everyone. Her mother looked around, the attendants turned their heads, and the guests looked puzzled. Connie turned her head and saw that Jaeda's parents had crooked, funny smiles on their faces. And, her dad grinned.

What was happening? Would something spoil her beautiful wedding? Suddenly she knew.
Little Jake raced down the aisle with a ribbon dangling from his tiny mouth. He rushed to Jaeda and sat like a mini sentry with his Min-Pin butt quivering. Jaeda pulled a dog treat from his pocket in exchange for the ribbon holding the ring. Jake seemed satisfied and laid down at Jaeda's feet and sighed.

Connie guffawed. Did brides laugh during their wedding ceremonies? This one did.

They exchanged rings and kissed after being pronounced husband and wife. Jaeda picked up Jake and tucked him under his arm while leading Connie back up the aisle with his other one.

Connie stopped halfway up, turned to Jaeda and kissed him fully on the lips. "I love you!" she said loud enough for all to hear.

Everyone clapped. Jake woofed.

~

Jill grinned. She had pulled it off holding the little dog back until just the right moment. Someday she would write her memoir about the adventures of being a wedding coordinator.

The End

ABOUT THE AUTHOR

Bonnie Engstrom and her psychologist husband, Dave, live in Arizona near four of their six grandchildren. The other two live in Costa Rica where they surf. They share their Arizona home with Sam and Lola, their two rescued mutts in charge of the household.

Bonnie is passionate about Jesus, her husband, her grandchildren and romance writing. She writes exclusively for the Forget Me Not Romances division of Winged Publications. *Connie's Silver Shoes* is Book Four in The Candy Cane Girls Series set in Newport Beach, California.

Because she loves to include real people in her stories, you may "see" yourself in a future one.

When she isn't writing, she is either moderating two online prayer chains or driving grandchildren to activities or volunteering in their classrooms. Currently, she is attempting to grow orchids, and has been successful growing basil in abundance, both of which she coaxes to thrive in the Arizona heat.

After dinner she reads romance novels for relaxation, and just before bed she makes a snack of nachos using Cindy's secret ingredient in *Cindy's Perfect Dance*.

Bonnie can be reached via email at bengstrom@hotmail.com. Be sure to put BOOK in the subject line so your post doesn't float around in her junk folder. Her website is www.bonnieengstrom.com, and she can also be found occasionally on Face Book, although she's not very astute at it. You can sign up for her *Life on the Lake* quarterly newsletter on either one.

www.ingramcontent.com/pod-product-compliance
Lightning Source LLC
Chambersburg PA
CBHW051943170626
46808CB00007B/2466